GNOME-A-GEDDON

Also by K. A. HOLT

Red Moon Rising

GNOME-A-GEDDON

K. A. HOLT

art by Colin Jack

Margaret K. McElderry Books

New York   London   Toronto   Sydney   New Delhi

MARGARET K. McELDERRY BOOKS
An imprint of Simon & Schuster Children's Publishing Division
1230 Avenue of the Americas, New York, New York 10020
This book is a work of fiction. Any references to historical events, real people, or
real places are used fictitiously. Other names, characters, places, and events are
products of the author's imagination, and any resemblance to actual events or
places or persons, living or dead, is entirely coincidental.
Text copyright © 2017 by Kari Anne Holt
Jacket illustration copyright © 2017 by Colin Jack
All rights reserved, including the right of reproduction in whole or in part in any
form.
MARGARET K. McELDERRY BOOKS is a trademark of Simon & Schuster, Inc.
For information about special discounts for bulk purchases, please contact Simon &
Schuster Special Sales at 1-866-506-1949 or business@simonandschuster.com.
The Simon & Schuster Speakers Bureau can bring authors to your live event. For
more information or to book an event, contact the Simon & Schuster Speakers
Bureau at 1-866-248-3049 or visit our website at www.simonspeakers.com.
Book design by Sonia Chaghatzbanian
The text for this book was set in ITC Souvenir Std.
The illustrations for this book were rendered digitally.
Manufactured in the United States of America
0317 FFG
First Edition
10 9 8 7 6 5 4 3 2 1
CIP data for this book is available from the Library of Congress.
ISBN 978-1-4814-7845-8 (hardcover)
ISBN 978-1-4814-7847-2 (eBook)

**For Julie, my first companion
to worlds unknown**

GNOME-A-GEDDON

1

Lizzie is glowing. And when I say that, I don't mean her cheeks are rosy and her skin is dewy and all that junk, I mean she's *actually* glowing. Her lips are splattered with the guts of a green glow bracelet, and there are glowing streaks of purple and pink and green on her teeth, on her cheeks, in her hair, and inside her ears. It looks like a unicorn threw up on her face. Which is exactly what I tell her.

"Even with unicorn barf on me, I look better than you do. What were you thinking, Buck?" She pokes my cheek with her finger and makes her badger face. It's the one where she scrunches up her nose so that her front two teeth stick out in obvious disgust. I swat away her finger. She's totally ruining my makeup.

Yes, makeup.

Everyone in line has some kind of face paint, even the boys, thankyouverymuch. I don't know anyone who would show up tonight *without* a costume.

"At least my makeup said 'nontoxic' on it," I say. "Not 'rinse off immediately if contents come in contact with skin.' You're going to get face rot or something."

A kid in front of us turns around, crossing his arms over the suede vest he's wearing. "I think she looks cool."

"As do I, dude," I say to the kid, who is easily half my width and twice my height. I have had my underwear pulled over my head by guys much smaller than this dude. "I'm just worried about the future of her beautiful face. You know . . ." I barely tilt my head toward a lady standing near the kid and make a "yikes" face. The lady is taller than he is, which seems like a physical impossibility. She's wearing a small crown made of bones—the signature crown of the Troll Queen. She keeps checking her phone. I think, if she wanted to, she could store her phone in one of her forehead wrinkles. She rubs the bridge of her nose and taps her foot just like my mom does when I'm telling her about the extra life cycles I just earned in the *Triumphant Gnome Syndicate* massive multiplayer online game.

The kid's eyes narrow. "That's my mom, dude. I made

her crown myself." He smiles, which, combined with his still-narrowed eyes, makes me wish I had my Troll Vanquishing Mace with me. If it existed in real life.

Lizzie laughs and it sounds like the most musical shattering glass ever.

"Oh," I say. "That crown is, um, awesome. You must have killed a lot of squirrels to get that just right." The kid looks at me like I just farted in his ear.

"I made it from chicken wings."

"Right," I say. "Yes. Of course." This is why I don't engage actual humans in conversation very often. I scratch at my makeup. The kid stares at me. I crane my neck for a view inside the bookstore. "Uh . . . wow, look at all those books!" The kid shakes his head and turns around.

The huge plate glass window is plastered with posters: HAROLD MACINAW'S GNOME-A-GEDDON: BOOK THREE IN THE TRIUMPHANT GNOME SYNDICATE SERIES! they say. IT'S ABOUT GNOME TIME. Past the posters I see huge stacks of the books. It makes my heart race just knowing they're in there. T-minus 20 minutes until I get my hands on one. So worth the seven-and-a-half-hour wait so far, even if it feels like my feet might fall off.

"If you really wanted to look like Maori," Lizzie says, sticking a fluorescent finger in my face, "you would have done this part better." She messes with the lines over my eyes and I know there's no way I still look like the Fisherman Gnome, whose magical fishhook can catch any enemy with the flick of a wrist. I look like Buck, the Pale, Brown-Haired, Smeary-Faced Kid with Aluminum Foil Hanging Off a String, who can recite almost every passage of the Triumphant Gnome Syndicate books by memory and has only one friend (not counting online friends).

There are other Maoris in line with us, but he's not the most popular gnome tonight. That, of course, is Custard, Teenage Gnome of the West. He really kicked butt in book two, *Little Big Gnome*. There are like a million Custards in line, all with their chaps and enchanted whips. If I get smacked in the face one more time, someone's going to get an enchanted whip stuffed up their nose. Or my imagination is going to stuff an enchanted whip up their nose, at least.

The kid turns back around, smacking me in the face with his enchanted whip. I force a smile. "Pardon *me*."

"Did you guys hear that Harold Macinaw is supposed to be here tonight?" the kid asks.

Lizzie's eye sparkle, but then she sighs. "I heard that," she says. "But it seems more likely unicorns will appear and give us all rides home."

"But will they be *barfing* unicorns?" I ask, jabbing Lizzie in the side with my elbow and waggling my too-loose glasses with my nose.

She ignores me. "I don't know why he would show up at midnight here, when he's some old codger who lives out in a hobbit hole in England somewhere."

"I would sell my left eyeball to meet the guy," I say, and the kid turns his attention from Lizzie. He thrusts his fist at me and I flinch, but then I realize he's going in for a bump. Our deep respect for Harold Macinaw has apparently trumped my insulting his mom.

Lizzie slides back down to where she's been sitting all night, on a Custard sleeping bag. She has books one and two with her and we've been reading our favorite passages out loud. I reach down for my soda. It's my fourth one for the night because I plan to stay up as long as it takes to finish the book in one sitting. Caffeine powers, activate!

We've been waiting so long for *Gnome-a-geddon*, I can't believe it's almost in my hands. It is sheer torture to finish a book and know you won't get to read the next one in the series for years. YEARS. Kids like my sister Willy have no idea what it's like. These books have always existed for her because she's so young. She just finished book two like a month ago, so she thinks Harold Macinaw just cranks out a new book for her when she's ready. But in actual, *grown-up kid world*, it takes EONS.

When you finish a Triumphant Gnome Syndicate book, it's like you're hungry—like actually starving—for more of the story. How are the gnomes going to vanquish the Troll Queen? And what about Custard's possibly mortal wound? You're just supposed to go on with your life, do everyday things, go to school, thwart online goblin raids, and wait TWO YEARS to find out the answers to these mysteries?

It's enough to make your head explode.

"Can I see your phone?" I ask Lizzie. She sighs but hands it over. I think she would hate it less if I asked to borrow her front teeth. One time—*one time*—I dropped her phone (and then accidentally kicked it, and then watched it slide into a storm drain, and then had to go with her to ask her mom to replace it), and now she treats it like it's made of goblin gold.

I click over to the browser and open up the website, TheHighCouncil.com. They've been counting down until *Gnome-a-geddon*'s release and it gives me a little zing when I see the counter blinking 00:00:00:15:31. 00:00:00:15:30. 00:00:00:15:29.

TheHighCouncil.com has been my lifeline these past two years, with so many friends on the message boards to help keep the spoilers away, and with the game where we can act out battles and strategies to get rid of the Troll Queen once and for all. I've even earned an exact replica of Master Hob's Troll Vanquishing Mace. It's worth five hit points and it's the best weapon ever for wiping out trolls.

Lizzie snaps her fingers for her phone back. She doesn't want to use it, I bet. She just doesn't want me to have it anymore. The green on her lips has smeared to her teeth, so the inside of her mouth glows as she rapid-fire quizzes the kid in front of us about Gnome trivia. If her mom saw her with all this obviously nonorganic, potentially poisonous stuff on her face she would faint dead away. Lizzie isn't even allowed to wear nonorganic T-shirts.

"Explain my costume—in a hundred words or less," she demands, pointing at the kid. The kid furrows his brow.

Easy. Lizzie isn't dressed like a gnome. She's dressed like a magical object. The least-favorite gnome of all is Johnny O'Sprocket, the Gnome of the Clouds. It's not that everybody is anticlouds, it's that (a) Johnny O'Sprocket is a ridiculous name and (b) his magical talisman is a horn that shoots rainbows. What do you do with a horn that shoots rainbows? Apparently, you use it to distract people from their intended path, so that they follow pretty rainbows away from wherever they actually want to go. See? Lame.

But Lizzie loves the idea of shooting rainbows, so she's painted herself up as a rainbow that is supposedly flying through the air. Right.

"Um, what did that weird kid say?" the kid asks, looking right at me but acting as if I'm invisible. "Are you unicorn barf?" Lizzie slugs him in the leg, leaving a glowing streak.

A horn sounds by the doors of the bookstore and everyone cheers.

"The Conch of the Syndicate!" someone shouts. Another cheer surges through the crowd. I'm sweating and my heart is beating like I'm in the middle of my own surprise party. I can't believe *Gnome-a-geddon* is *finally* coming out!

A figure climbs slowly up a ladder in front of the bookstore. He's holding a huge seashell and wearing a red pointy hat, in the traditional costume of Maori. Instead of having his face painted, though, he's wearing a mask.

The short guy on the ladder tosses the conch into the crowd and there's a mad scrum over who gets it. Then he reaches up and pulls off his mask.

The crowd gasps, just like people always do in movies, and everyone goes silent.

The man smiles.

I look at Lizzie. Her mouth opens and closes like a fish's.

"Is that . . . ?" I whisper.

"I think . . . ," she replies.

"It's Harold Macinaw!" someone screams. "It's really him!"

The crowd surges forward and a group of bookstore workers struggles to keep everyone from accidentally toppling the ladder.

Macinaw holds up a hand and everyone quiets down.

"Surprise!" he says, with a big friendly smile, his poofy gray beard almost hiding it but his eyes giving it away. "I wanted to sneak by tonight just to tell everyone how grateful I am that you love the books. I hope you'll love this next book just as—"

There's a huge flash and a bang and a giant cloud of stinking, choking smoke. People scream, and I grab Lizzie's arm as she stumbles back into me. There's another bang and I know this isn't part of the book release. Something is happening. My first thought (other than *Please don't have us all die*) is how glad I am that Mom didn't let Willy come with us. This is not a good way to introduce someone to a book release party, especially an eight-year-old prone to chewing her fingertips raw at the thought of crowds of people. Screaming crowds of trampling nerds would *definitely* freak her out.

Time slows and I see people running, screaming, dropping fake enchanted whips on the sidewalk as they flee. I spin around, trying to figure out what's going on. Macinaw isn't on the ladder anymore. I can't even see the ladder anymore. My ears are ringing from the noise, my heart racing. But there's no debris. If it had been an explosion, there would be stuff flying everywhere, right?

Lizzie is staring at me, her huge golden eyes wider than I've ever seen them. Most of the crowd is stampeding down the street now, though some people are hiding behind the trees along the parking lot and some are huddled around the fallen ladder. The book release banner in front of the store is hanging perilously by one corner, drifting in the breeze. Sirens howl in the distance. The bookstore workers look just as stunned as I feel.

Lizzie grabs my hand and we rush over to the ladder. I expect to see Macinaw lying there, unconscious at the very least, but when we push our way through the small crowd, we see . . . nothing.

No one is under the ladder. Just a pointy hat and a mask.

"Where is he?" I ask a bookstore employee. She turns and stares at me, her eyes vacant.

"I don't know," she says. "He just . . . disappeared."

2

We climb into Lizzie's car, practically hyperventilating from running so fast. Her mom is asleep up against the steering wheel. Even the slamming of car doors doesn't wake her up.

"Mom!" Lizzie yells. "MOM!"

Lizzie's mom snuffles awake and rubs a hand over her face. There's a red imprint of the steering wheel on her forehead that looks like a frowny face.

"Hey," she says, waking up. "Have fun?" There's a pause, then . . . "What's on your FACE?!"

Oops. In all the craziness we forgot to wipe off the one hundred percent nonorganic glowing gunk.

Lizzie's eyebrows go sky-high as she wipes at her face

with her sleeve. The glowing smears stand out against her dark skin. "Didn't you hear the explosions? Something happened!"

"Explosions?!" Now Lizzie's mom is really awake. "Oh my God, Lizzie, are you guys okay?" She swings her body around the front seat and turns on the small overhead light. She grabs Lizzie's arms one at a time and looks them over.

"We're fine, Mom," Lizzie says, yanking her arms away. "But Harold Macinaw is gone! He just disappeared."

A fire truck races by.

"Buck?" Lizzie's mom puts her hand on my cheek. "Okay? Yeah?"

I nod. This is all so weird. It can't be real, can it?

I stand in my dark driveway and say good night to Lizzie while her mom idles the car along the curb.

"Do you think he's okay?" Lizzie asks, tears making her eyes glow almost as much as the leftover smeared paint on her face.

"I'm sure he's fine," I say, even though I'm not sure of any such thing. "It was probably some kind of crazy trick. With screaming. And fire trucks. Very elaborate for the sake of the dorks, you know. So we'd fall for whatever prank he's—"

Lizzie blinks three times (her signal to me whenever she thinks I'm going on and on about something) and puts her hand on my arm. I stop talking.

"We didn't get our books," Lizzie says, and I realize she's right. After all that, my brain hadn't even registered that I don't have the new book to read tonight. All that caffeine gone to waste. How am I going to sleep now?

"We can go get them tomorrow," I answer. "I'm sure someone will take us back to the bookstore."

Lizzie shakes her head. "Mom's never going to let me go back. Not after explosions."

"We'll take our bikes," I say. "It's not that far. We'll just tell our folks we're going to the park, or whatever. And you'll have your phone in case they need us."

My mom won't let me have a phone. It's the worst thing ever. I can't even talk about it right now.

Lizzie nods. "Okay. I'll come by in the morning. Say hey to Willy for me."

"Sure," I say. "Well . . . good night." We do our patented fist bump, fist bump, finger flare, fist bump.

"'Night," she says over her shoulder. Ms. Adams waits to drive away until I'm shutting the front door behind me.

"Hey, Buck," Mom says. Her dark curly hair flies out around her head in all directions. She's in her bathrobe and her glasses are on the tip of her nose, a magazine in her hand. Willy is halfway down the stairs, running so fast her red-tinged freckles might get left behind. Her curls are crazy, too, and she's wearing her Canopy, Gnome of the Rain Forest pajamas. She's holding Mom's e-reader. Mom preordered an electronic version of *Gnome-a-geddon* when she broke the news Willy couldn't come with us to the release party. I guess it must have downloaded right at midnight. Great. Now Willy gets to read it before me.

Seriously. WORST. NIGHT. EVER.

Mom looks me up and down. "Why are you so sweaty? Where's your book?"

Willy takes a few more steps down the stairs when she sees Mom isn't going to yell at her for being up so late. She puffs out her cheeks and makes whooshing motions with her arms, pretending to use Canopy's wind power to fly herself down to the couch.

"Was it great, Buck? Was everyone dressed up? Did they like your makeup? How many people were there?" Willy chews at her fingers and pulls her legs up under her, snuggling into the old orange afghan that is never not on the couch.

"Hey," I say, noticing the bulging pocket in her bathrobe. "HEY! Is that my copy of *A Tale of Gnomekind*?!" I reach over and yank it from her pocket. I've read it so many times the cover is hanging off. "I told you not to touch this! What if you tear it? What if it gets ruined? DON'T TOUCH MY STUFF, WILLY!"

Willy looks at me, bewildered. "I just wanted to read about how Custard got the whip, I just—" Her eyes are filling with tears. She makes me so crazy sometimes, doing stuff like this. Touching my things and then making *me* feel bad when I yell at her.

"I need everyone to calm down here," Mom says, sitting on the couch between us. "Buck, you need to take a deep breath. Tell Willy you're sorry for snapping at her. And Willy, don't be grabbing things out of Buck's room without his permission, okay?"

Willy says *okay* and I mutter *sorry* at the same time.

I get up and go get a drink of water, and then I tell them the whole story.

3

Willy and I are sitting on the front porch when Lizzie rides up on her bike.

"Could have been aliens," Willy says, looking up from the e-reader. "They have, like, beams and stuff they can use to just suck people onto their ships. Or maybe spies that another author hired. Spies are cool."

"Or maybe a space-time rip," I say, making a grab for the e-reader, but Willy is quick and she dodges me. "You never know when one of those is going to appear."

Willy's eyes narrow. "There's no such thing as a space-time rip, just like there's no such thing as real trolls." She chews on the corner of a finger as if deciding if she believes what she's said or not. "Right?"

"There's no such thing as trolls, Willy." I sigh. "If the book is too scary, you better just give it to me."

She spits out the fingernail and gives me a steely look when I reach for the e-reader again. "Mom said you can have it when I'm done, remember? Quit trying to steal it from me or I'm going to start reading the whole thing out loud."

"You wouldn't dare," I say, imitating her narrowed eyes.

Willy pulls a pencil out from behind her ear, where she always keeps a pencil handy. She pulls a small notepad from her back pocket and draws a stick figure of herself saying, "I dare. I always dare." She puts the pencil back behind her ear and holds the notepad in front of my face as she starts reading the e-book again.

I shove her slightly and she bonks into Mom's pot of tomato plants, spilling soil onto the porch, and spilling my copy of *A Tale of Gnomekind* out of her other pocket.

"Willy! Dude! You can't keep stealing my book!" I make a grab for it, trying not to rip the precariously dangling cover.

Lizzie drops her bike in the grass and walks over. "Whatcha doing?"

Willy says, "We're just trying to figure out what happened to Harold Macinaw. And Buck's trying to steal the book from me."

"She stole *my* book!" I point at her accusingly.

Lizzie's eyebrows go up and she glances down at the e-reader. "You have *Gnome-a-geddon* on there?"

"It's two against one now. You better run, little girl!" I stand up and make another grab for the e-reader.

"Buck! You're going to break it!" Willy screeches. "I hope you get swallowed by a space-time rip! Or eaten by trolls!" She cuddles the e-reader like a baby, grabs my old *A Tale of Gnomekind,* and runs for the tree house.

"Ah, I can feel the worry for Macinaw filling the air," Lizzie says, rolling her eyes and laughing.

I reach under the porch swing and grab the cold sodas I stashed earlier. I hand one to Lizzie and drop one into the deep pocket on the leg of my cargo pants.

"Oh, thanks!" she says, twisting off the cap. She takes a long chug, then wipes her mouth with the back of her hand. "You will never believe the stuff Mom bought yesterday. Beet juice and seltzer water. 'We can make our own sodas now!'" She does a perfect impression of her mom and it makes me laugh every time. "I almost barfed."

Lizzie's mom isn't such a bad person, she just thinks everything in the world is out to kill everyone.

I give Lizzie a bag of Cheez Flairs to go with the soda. I'm afraid if I don't give her some "supplements" of my own, she's going to turn into a leaf or something.

My cruddy old bike is in the middle of the driveway where I left it yesterday. Luckily Dad is out of town or he would have run over it when he got home from work. Though maybe if he had, I'd get a new, less cruddy bike.

"Where are you guys going?" Willy yells down from the tree house. She pulls her Silly Putty out of her pocket and cracks some bubbles. It's supposed to help her stop chewing at her fingers, but sometimes I see her forget and try to eat the Silly Putty.

"Nowhere," I say.

"Fine, don't tell me," she says. "I'll just have more quiet time to read *Gnome-a-geddon*." Her lips curl into a smile just like the Grinch's. She waves the e-reader at me. "See you later!"

I give her a look that says it all.

"Stay out as long as you want," she says. "I don't care. Maybe I'll finish when you're gone and we can talk about what happens at the end. Except—you won't know because you haven't read it yet!" She cackles and I try to hide a laugh. The spark in her eyes tells me just how much she loves the fact that she's reading the book before me. And even though I want to strangle her, I can sort of see how it must be nice for her to have something to hold over my head. A little-sister win—for a little while, at least.

"Does Mom know you're leaving?" she asks.

"She will when you tell her, I guess," I say, giving her my best big-brother smile. I kick my leg over my bike and hop on.

"She doesn't like you running off!" Willy yells after us. "You better get back soon!"

I raise my hand in a wave, and soon we're far enough that I can't hear what she's hollering at us. How can an eight-year-old be such a worrywart? It's one of the reasons I *call* her Willy. She has the willies more than anyone I've ever known. Well, that and her actual name is Wilma. Poor kid.

"Why didn't you steal the e-reader from her while she was asleep last night?" Lizzie asks as she pumps her bike ahead of me.

"Believe me, I tried," I say, already out of breath. My cruddy bike is not a fancy ten-speed like Lizzie's. "She hid it somewhere good. I was ready to turn her room inside out when Mom came in and was all, 'You better go to bed before I freak out!' so I had to give up."

"Lame," Lizzie says, and I don't know if she means me or Mom. Maybe both.

We pedal up over a hill (well, Lizzie pedals and I grunt and heave) and when we get to the top I see that there's no way we're getting our books today. Not from this bookstore, at least.

"What is all that?" Lizzie asks, squinting ahead of us.

I straighten my glasses and it all comes into focus. "Police tape," I say.

The yellow tape is all around the front of the bookstore like it's some kind of off-season haunted house. A couple of cruisers are in the parking lot, but their lights aren't flashing.

We pedal up to the edge of the tape. "Look," I say. There's a handwritten sign taped on the door. Lizzie and I lean our bikes against a light pole and walk over to the crime scene tape. The cops are in the parking lot talking to some bookstore employees. I hold the tape up and sneak under it. When I turn I see that Lizzie hasn't followed. Her eyes are darting from me to the police cars and back to me again.

"What are you doing?" she whispers.

"It must be my 'lack of impulse control because of perfectly normal late development of my prefrontal cortex.'"

I'm parroting what the lady who smelled like bologna told my mom two years ago in an after-school meeting. The meeting ended with Mom taking me out for a milk shake and telling me that sometimes, ironically, schools are not always the best places for smart kids.

I motion for Lizzie to follow me, and she finally does, but not without blinking at me and sighing deeply. Now that we're closer I can see that the sign on the door says, CLOSED DUE TO UNFORESEEN INCIDENT. WE WILL REOPEN AS SOON AS POSSIBLE.

Henry, the store owner, is banging his hands on an old truck and yelling at the cops. I can only catch a few of the words, like "Biggest sales day besides the day after Thanksgiving!" and "We've told you everything!" He's keeping the police busy as he rants and shakes his arms, so I sneak closer to the fallen ladder. There are little cards with numbers on them next to the pointy hat and the mask. There's a number by the ladder, too. Lizzie yelps and I turn as she almost trips on one last numbered card. It's next to a little splash of something red just a few feet away from the ladder, near where she's standing behind me.

"Is that . . . ?" Lizzie swallows hard.

My brain is screaming *OH MY GOD, HAROLD MAC-INAW'S BLOOD IS ON THE SIDEWALK,* but I try to play it cool. "I don't know." I lean down for a closer look. It could definitely be blood. But it could also be an old stain or paint or anything.

Lizzie's phone rings and we both jump. She swipes the screen to answer it and I feel that itchy feeling I always get when I can't believe she has a phone and I don't.

She says "Uh-huh" and "Okay" a bunch of times and then hangs up.

"Come on," she says. "That was your mom. She's mad. She wants you back now." Lizzie starts jog-walking back to our bikes. I throw one more look over my shoulder at the crime scene. Is it really a crime scene? Did someone commit a crime against Harold Macinaw? Could it have been an accident? A stunt?

"Hey!" someone yells. "You kids! Get away from there!"

My head whips around and I see one of the cops jogging over to us.

"Yep," I say to the back of Lizzie's head. "Definitely time to go." We pick up the pace, and soon we're flying back down the street on our bikes.

"What was that?" Lizzie asks when I manage to pedal alongside her.

"I call it running. I know it looks more like flopping and squealing, but—"

"No, Buck," she says with a laugh. "All the little numbered cards."

"It's like crime scene investigation stuff," I say. If her
mom let her watch TV, she'd know these kinds of important CSI details.

"You saw that red drop," I say.

Lizzie changes gears and slows to my speed.

"It looked an awful lot like blood," I say.

Lizzie's mouth falls open a bit. "You really think someone was trying to hurt Harold Macinaw? The smartest
koala bear of a man who's ever existed?"

I shrug. "I don't want to think that, but I didn't see him
eating a red Popsicle up there, did you?"

"I don't believe it," Lizzie says. "Maybe there really was
a space-time rip."

"I wish," I say. "A space-time rip right here in this small
town? Maybe we could take a trip to Narnia or find some
planet where people actually like chubby kids who play too
many video games."

"You're not just a chubby kid who plays too many video
games, Buck," Lizzie says. We're almost home now, which
is good because my shirt is soaked with sweat. "You're
smart enough to have every stinkin' word of every Triumphant Gnome Syndicate book memorized."

"Well, I don't know if that's smart or just one more sign I'm a superdork with an extra helping of nerd." I drop my bike into the front yard and drop myself down to lie in the grass for a minute. "I hope Mom isn't too mad. It would be really nice if she'd drive us to another bookstore somewhere."

Lizzie lies down next to me. "Well, we *are* the only two people in the world who haven't read the new book yet. Maybe she'll take pity on us." She closes her eyes. "Do you feel guilty for still wanting to read it so bad now that Macinaw is . . . missing?"

"Do you?" I ask. "The whole world could be on fire from an epic troll attack and I would still want to bury myself in a hole and read the entire book cover to cover. Is that awful?"

"Nah, I don't think so." Lizzie stands up and holds out her hand. "Let's go see if your mom really will take pity on us."

We walk through the front door and straight into the kitchen, where I gulp down a glass of water like I've just returned from a ten-mile bike ride instead of a two-mile one. Mom comes downstairs holding a box. She puts it on the kitchen table.

"Where have you guys been?" she asks. She has that

Mom look—the one where I can't tell if she's about to freak or just give me a warning. I shrug while Lizzie admits we went back to the store to get books, even after all the scary stuff that happened last night.

Mom doesn't look disappointed in me like I thought she might. She just gives this half smile. She pulls two brand-new copies of *Gnome-a-geddon* out of the box and hands one to each of us.

"I preordered these with Willy's. I figured a couple of extra copies never hurt." Mom smiles. "They arrived this morning, but you left before I could give them to you." Mom's smile turns stern. How does she do that so fast?

"Sorry," Lizzie and I say at the same time. Then Lizzie lunges at Mom and hugs her tight, knocking her off-balance a little. "Thank you, thank you, thank you, Mrs. Rogers! I promise to read it as fast as possible and give it right back."

Mom laughs. "No rush, Lizzie, take your time." She reaches over and ruffles my hair. "I know this one over here will have it done by tomorrow. I'll get it from him."

"Oh no you won't," I say with a smile. "I'll have it read by the morning, but then I have to read again for details. You better figure out Willy's hiding place so you can read her copy."

Mom shakes her head, laughing. "You guys start reading. Who wants lunch? I'll heat up a pizza."

"Gross, nonorganic, made-of-cardboard-and-chemicals pizza?" Lizzie asks.

Mom sighs and nods.

"Yes!" Lizzie claps. "You're the best, Mrs. Rogers!"

We both give her the most grateful smiles in the history of grateful smiles and sprint upstairs.

"Keep the door open!" Mom shouts after us. "And don't ever disappear without telling me where you're going again, okay?"

"Okay!" I yell down the stairs. "Sorry again. And thanks again! You're the best mom in the whole world. In the whole universe!"

We run past Willy's room and I see her splayed across her bed, holding the e-reader over her face. I better hurry or she's going to torture me with spoilers. I toss myself on my bed and Lizzie scrunches into the beanbag chair by the window.

Gnome-a-geddon.

This is it!

Lizzie gives a little squeal and I laugh. Then all my attention goes to the book, starting with the cover.

Custard's face looks tired. I knew it would. I've been

seeing the cover for months online and on TV. But up close I can see the lines in his face, the redness of his eyes. *Gnome-a-geddon* is intense and I haven't even cracked the spine yet. Custard's face is warped, stretched thin in the fish-eye lens of Johnny O'Sprocket's spyglass. The lens is the biggest image on the cover, with O'Sprocket blurry in the background, standing on a hill. I rub my hand over the cover, feeling the slightly raised words of the title.

I've spent two years waiting for this moment.

I close my eyes and take a deep breath. The spine crackles as I open the book and start reading.

On the shores of a foreign land, Custard awakens to the sound of footsteps. . . .

I close the book, wide-eyed. Four a.m.

Holy trolls, that was a heckuva thing.

I tiptoe downstairs and grab the phone off the kitchen table. I bring it back to my room and dial Lizzie's mobile number. She answers on the first ring.

"Have you finished yet?" I ask.

"Not yet. So close, though. Oh my gosh, Buck! I just . . . I can't . . . It's . . ."

I laugh. "I know. I know. It's even more amazing than I thought it would be."

I hear her yawning.

"Hurry up and finish and then go to bed. I'm in agony to talk to you about it, but I want to do it face-to-face."

"You're the bestest friend ever, Buck Rogers."

"Yeah, yeah, just get some sleep and then get over here!"

"Sounds like a plan," she answers.

I hang up, my mind racing. How in the world am I going to sleep? So much has just happened. The Troll Queen is out of control. Even Canopy, who is against teaming up with *anyone* (she's such a loner!), is willing to assemble a full army against her—and assembling armies has been illegal for centuries!

The whole story is changing now. My brain is spinning.

I climb off my bed and walk over to the window. I open it just a bit so that the night air washes over my face. It's warm and humid and makes me just the tiniest bit drowsy. I open the window a little more and stick my head all the way out, close my eyes, and take in a big breath. When I open my eyes I see a figure walking down the sidewalk. It looks exactly like Lizzie.

I rub my eyes. The figure walks under the streetlight and confirms what I first thought.

"Liz-zie!" I hiss out the window. It can't be anyone but her. No one in the world looks like Lizzie, except for Lizzie, with her dandelion poof hair and those crazy long, long legs. "Hey! What are you doing down there?!" Was she already out on the sidewalk when I called her just now? I could have sworn she was at home reading.

She doesn't look up, just keeps walking slowly away.

"Lizzie!" I whisper-shout out the window again, but she doesn't turn around. Why isn't she answering me?

I run down the stairs as quietly as I can and carefully open the front door, then close it behind me. I jog across the porch, through the damp front yard, and down the sidewalk. My bare feet make super-loud *Slap! Slap!* noises in the early-morning silence.

Thankfully, all the houses on our street are dark. There's no one around, except for Lizzie just a few feet ahead of me. "Lizzie," I say in a harsh whisper, putting my hand on her shoulder. "What are you doing out here?" She half-turns and stares just past me. Her eyes are blank, more light brown than their usual golden, like she's sleepwalking. Her hair has taken on an impressive Afro status.

I put my other hand on her other shoulder and turn her all the way around to face me. "Hey," I whisper even though I want to shout it. "What are you doing here?"

She doesn't answer. Her lips curl back, showing her teeth, sparkling in the moonlight. Her eyes are still dull and open too wide. Is that a smile? I let go of her shoulders and take a step back. She's really creeping me out.

"Do you want me to walk you home?" I ask.

She just keeps staring but then nods once. "I like to walk," she says, and for a second I think she's imitating a really loud robot. I wince and hold my finger to my lips. She holds her finger to her lips, too.

"Come on," I whisper, glancing back at my house. Still dark. It'll only take me ten minutes to walk to Lizzie's house and back. As long as Mom doesn't spontaneously decide to check in on me in the middle of the night, she'll never know I was gone.

We walk side by side. Lizzie has on a plain white T-shirt and blue gym shorts. I've never seen her in these clothes before, but maybe they're her pj's. I look down, just now realizing I'm in *my* pj's. Luckily, I went for a Triumphant Gnome Syndicate T-shirt and old cargo shorts instead of my usual underpants.

We get to her house and she turns to go up the front walk.

"Hey," I say. "Maybe we should go in the back? So we don't wake up your mom." She does that creepy smile again and we walk through the grass to the side of the house. I shake the gate like I learned to do years ago and the lock comes loose. She follows me into the backyard. I look up and see the light is still on in her room. This is all very weird.

I snap my fingers in front of her face and say, "Wake up," but she doesn't even blink. Maybe her mom gave her some kind of weird supplement and the side effects are "sleepwalking with eyes open" and "freaking out your best friend."

"This is the back," she says, in that same loud robot voice as before. I can hear it echoing off the walls of the neighboring houses.

"Shhh," I say. "Tone it down, Shouty McShouterpants."

"My name is Elizabeth Kathleen Adams," Lizzie says in her super-loud voice. "I live at 3201 Sycamore Street. My mother's name is Georgette. My father lives in Kenya."

I'm trying to cover her mouth while she's talking, my eyes going wider with every syllable. She's taller than me so I'm grabbing at the front and back of her head so I can keep my hand in place over her mouth. I have to get her inside.

She's still talking loudly through my hand—"I'm in the sixth grade at Columbia Middle School"—when my stomach creeps into my toenails. I hear the very familiar screeching of a window opening.

"Who's there?"

I can only imagine what this looks like: a kid, barefoot, in his pajamas, wrestling with a girl in her backyard at 4 a.m. I gulp air as I look up to see which window opened.

"Buck?"

Wait.

I squint. The light from the window is bright, so maybe I'm not seeing this right, but who else could it be?

"What are you doing down there? Who's that with you?" Lizzie leans half her body out the upstairs window. She's wearing her retainer so she kind of slurs when she talks.

I look down at the crook of my elbow, where I have successfully silenced the other Lizzie by getting her in a headlock. I look back up at the window.

"Uh," I say.

"Don't move," Lizzie from the window says. I see her race out of the room, the curtains fluttering out the window for a minute from the sudden movement.

In about two seconds, she's in the backyard, out of breath. The retainer makes her mouth kind of puff out as she sucks in the night air. I release the other Lizzie and they stare at each other.

"This . . . ," Lizzie says, trailing off. She reaches out and pokes the other Lizzie in the nose. The other Lizzie reaches out and does the same. "This does not compute,"

Lizzie whispers. She glances at me and I shrug.

"She was walking down the sidewalk outside my house. I thought she was you. Sleepwalking or something."

"Buck," Lizzie says, waving her hand in front of the other Lizzie's face. The other Lizzie copies her again. "BUCK!" she shouts.

"Shhhhhhh!" I say.

She puts both hands in her hair. "What is going ON?!" The other Lizzie puts her hands in her hair, too, and does that creepy smile.

"We have to get her inside," I say.

Lizzie looks at me like I've just turned bright purple. "We can't bring this . . . creature . . . *inside my house*! Haven't you *ever* watched a horror movie?!"

"We can't just leave her out here," I say. "What if she wanders off and robs a bank or eats a dog? People will think YOU did it!"

"Mom!" Lizzie says. "She'll know what to do." She whirls around and starts running back toward the house. I run after her, holding the other Lizzie's hand and pulling her behind me. I know I should be terrified about waking up a grown-up in the middle of the night and presenting some kind of alien twin of her daughter, but honestly? I can't wait to see the look on her face.

We burst into the house and Lizzie runs to her mom's room. I stand in the bedroom doorway, with the other Lizzie next to me. She's looking around, running her hands over the dark wood that frames the doorway.

"Do you have a television set?" she asks suddenly. Her voice sounds even louder and robot-i-er in the quiet of the house. "I would enjoy watching many television shows that include ninjas." I clap my hand over her mouth.

The lump in the bed doesn't move.

"Mom!" Lizzie says, shaking her. "Mom!" She still doesn't move. Lizzie looks up at me and her eyes have that look in them like a dog that has just accidentally fallen in a swimming pool after trying to catch a ball.

I go over to the bed, my heart galloping up my throat.

Lizzie's mom appears to be sound asleep, but she's absolutely rigid. Like she's frozen. I put my hand on her forehead. She feels warm, not too hot, just right.

"Ms. Adams," I say, leaning over her face. I push her shoulder. "Ms. Adams!" She doesn't move at all. She just looks like she's sleeping soundly.

"Okay," I say, even though things are obviously not okay at all. "Let's think."

I run into the bathroom, fill up a cup of water, and come back in the room.

"Buck? What are you—"

I throw the cup of water into Ms. Adams's face. She doesn't even flinch.

"Buck!" Lizzie shouts, and shoves me.

"What?" I say. "If that doesn't wake her up, nothing will. Did she take a pill or something?"

"I don't know," Lizzie says. "I don't think she takes pills for anything ever. She has, like, a thing against pills."

The other Lizzie is picking up framed pictures off the chest of drawers. "My mom and I enjoy fishing," she says. "My favorite food is a juicy cheeseburger."

"You're a vegetarian, you space alien!" Lizzie shouts at her. "You haven't had a cheeseburger in over a year!"

"Okay, okay," I say, holding Lizzie back as she attempts to pounce on the fake Lizzie. "Let's all go to my house. Mom will know what to do." I wonder if anyone, anywhere, could know what to do in such a weird situation.

"Maybe we should call 911," Lizzie says. Her forehead wrinkles and she chews at her bottom lip.

"To report what?" I try not to sound impatient. "A fake you and a grown-up who's sleeping through the whole thing? The police are going to think we're joking around with them."

"This is not a joke," Lizzie says. She puts her hand on her mom's hand.

"I know," I say. "*I* don't think it's a joke. Come on." I grab Lizzie's hand. "Let's go see what Mom thinks we should do." Lizzie takes the other Lizzie's hand and we walk quickly out of the house and back into the night.

"Do you have any video game systems?" the other Lizzie asks in her crazytown voice. "Shooting games are boss."

"Just ignore her," I say, picking up speed. I don't want to talk to a space alien twin about how my parents enjoy torturing me by not only refusing to buy me a mobile phone, but also refusing to buy me any video game consoles. At least I have a laptop and Triumphant Gnome Syndicate game.

We race down the sidewalk and cut through my yard. We burst into the house and up the stairs. I peek into Willy's room and she's bundled under the covers, still sound asleep. I tiptoe in and poke her. She groans and flips over. Okay. Good. Not paralyzed or whatever like Lizzie's mom. I sneak back out when I see Willy's still sound asleep.

In the hall, I give Lizzie a thumbs-up and she mouths, *Whew.* I take a deep breath before opening the door to Mom and Dad's room. Dad is still out of town and I know Mom hates to be woken up. But this is a true emergency, so . . .

"Mom," I whisper. I wipe the sweat from my forehead and turn my head to the side so I can be face-to-face with her. "Mom. Wake up." She doesn't move. "Mom!" I say loudly, thinking of the one thing that would definitely wake her. "I just threw up all over my bed!" She still doesn't move. Lizzie walks over and gives her a push. Just like Lizzie's mom, Mom is rigid. She's warm and breathing, but frozen. So, grown-ups are frozen in the beds, but kids aren't. What is going on?

"Maybe you have a handheld console?" the other Lizzie says loudly, looking from me to Lizzie. "A small device with games of fighting?"

"Come on," I say. "My room." As we walk out of Mom's room I flip on the hall light. Not that I'm scared, but you know . . . light keeps your brain cells more engaged.

Lizzie and the other Lizzie follow me across the hall. I turn the light on in my room and HOLY WHOA!

Sitting in my chair at my desk, fiddling with my laptop, is someone with very familiar brown curly hair, very familiar squinty brown eyes hidden behind glasses, and very familiar chubby cheeks flushed pink. I see . . . me.

5

Lizzie screams. The other me looks up from the laptop and smiles the same kind of dead smile as the other Lizzie.

"Oh, hello," He/I says. "I am trying to find some personal computer games to play. It is unfortunate there are no gaming consoles in this household." Fake Lizzie's eyebrows go up; then she smiles and walks to him.

"Perhaps we can figure this out together." They lean over the laptop and I pull Lizzie out of my room. I shut the door and wish I had some way to lock them in there.

"What in Hob's pants is going on, Buck?" Lizzie asks as we go downstairs.

"Even space alien fake versions of us think I should have

an Xbox!" I shout, flopping into a chair at the kitchen table and banging my head on the table. I lay my cheek on the cold Formica and look up at her. "I don't think this has anything to do with Hob's pants, though." She forces a smile.

Hob, the old gnome from the Macinaw books, is known for losing—and hiding—magical objects in his pockets. We don't seem to be losing anything tonight. We do seem to be gaining things, though.

"Buck?" The front door squeaks open.

Lizzie and I swing around to face the door.

Dad!

I forgot he was taking an overnight flight to get home from his business trip. He walks in, pulling a wheelie suitcase and looking tired and rumpled. He drops his briefcase by the long table next to the front door and wheels his suitcase up against the wall. He kicks off his shoes and sighs like it's the best feeling ever in the whole wide world to not be wearing shoes. Then he comes over and rumples my hair. "How ya doing? You're up early, huh?"

"Dad, we—"

"Mr. Rogers! There's—"

Lizzie and I are yelling at the same time.

"I just spent six hours on a red-eye flight back home,"

Dad says, putting a hand to the bridge of his nose. "Can there please be less shouting?" He loosens his tie and pulls a water bottle from the fridge. "You know what it's like to spend three days at a conference where the only thing anyone talks about is selling corrugated cardboard?"

We shake our heads.

"It stinks. That's what it's like. I just want quiet and a soft bed." He frowns. "Does Lizzie's mom know she's here so early—or is it late?" He eyes me suspiciously.

"She . . . she knows," I say. "But Dad, the thing is . . ." I don't even know how to say it. There are space alien fake versions of me and Lizzie upstairs? Mom won't wake up?

Dad takes a step toward me and opens his mouth to say something but suddenly freezes in place.

Lizzie's hand covers her mouth.

"Dad?" I whisper, waving my hand in front of his face. He's absolutely motionless, his eyes staring, unblinking.

Lizzie and I both stand there for probably a full minute, just staring at Dad. What should we do? We could call the police, but what would they say? If Mom and Dad are frozen and Lizzie's mom is frozen, wouldn't they put us in some kind of quarantine to see if we've all been contaminated with an alien virus? What would they do with the extra Buck and Lizzie?

A cold feeling slithers into my stomach. If our parents are sick or messed up, the police will take us away to an orphanage or something. Maybe even send Willy to one place and me to another. That's what happens in movies. I swallow hard.

"Let's go wake up Willy," I say. "We'll go see Henry at the bookstore. He never leaves that place."

Lizzie lifts her upper lip in that oh-so-familiar badger face. "Why would we go see *Henry*?"

I shrug. "He's smart and a little bit crazy and if we tell him what's going on, I don't think he'll turn us over to the police or child protective services or anything. Plus, whenever I have a question about something I can pretty much always find the answer at the bookstore."

Lizzie blinks three times and says, "Okay. But I'm not agreeing because I think you're right, I'm only agreeing because I don't know what else to do and it is super-creepy in this house right now."

I nod and head up the stairs. We burst into Willy's room. She's still all bundled up under the covers.

I shake her shoulder and say, "Willy. Wake up."

"My name is Wilma Rogers," Willy says, sitting up and nearly bonking foreheads with me. "I enjoy climbing trees and reading books. My favorite food is macaroni and cheese. Do you have any video games I can play?"

I stagger back and grab hold of the dresser to steady myself. She's just like Fake Buck and Fake Lizzie. But if this is Fake Willy, then . . . where's the real Willy?

"WILLY!" I shout, running downstairs. "WILLY, where are you?!"

Lizzie runs after me. I spin in circles in the living room, trying to figure things out.

"If we're here, and our fake selves are upstairs, and Willy's fake self is upstairs . . .where is the real Willy?" My heart threatens to fly out of the top of my head.

"She can't be far, Buck," Lizzie says, putting a hand on my shoulder to stop me from twirling around. "We'll go right now and find her."

"She can't be out there on her own, Lizzie. She gets worried when the light is on too long in the bathroom. She's got to be freaking out right now."

The more I think about Willy out by herself somewhere, the more I sweat. And the more I sweat, the more I—hey.

"Do you hear that?" I ask Lizzie. "A kind of roaring water noise?"

Lizzie moves her eyes around, as if that would help her hear anything. Then her eyes go wide. "Yeah, actually. I think I do."

We stand next to each other for a minute and listen. All I can think about is the ocean. So soothing. And rhythmic. And calming. I love the ocean. We should totally go to the ocean right now.

Lizzie walks past me and right out the front door. I follow. She must know the way to the ocean. We can stand in the waves together. Watch some birds. Yes. The ocean.

We're walking down the middle of the street now and somewhere deep inside me is a little voice shouting. I can barely hear it over the soothing noise of the ocean waves. "What are you doing?!" the tiny voice shouts. "This is weird. Snap out of it, dummy!" But then I see a long line of other kids. They must be going to the ocean just like me. I better get in line with them. The water is going to be so blue. And think about how nice it will be to just lie in the sand and—

OW! SON OF A STARFISH!

I'm on my knees in the middle of the street, and it feels like a lightning bolt has just shot through my brain. Lizzie is facedown on the asphalt, groaning. A tiny man with a black beard, scruffy clothes, and some kind of chopstick thing in his hand is standing over us, breathing fast and hard. The line of kids is marching away from us and around the street corner.

"Hey, man!" I yell, staggering to my feet. Lights flash in front of my eyes and I think I might pass out. I reach out toward him and smack the chopstick out of his hand. It hits the ground and breaks in half. "What did you do to us?" I can't decide if I'm angrier about not going to the beach or about the searing pain between my eyes.

The man scrambles to the ground, grabbing at the broken pieces of the chopstick. "What did I do? WHAT DID I DO? Look at what YOU just did!" He throws the pieces of the chopstick at me. They bounce off my waist. That's how short this dude is.

"I've only been saving you for five point two seconds and you've already jeopardized the entire plan!" the man shouts as he leans over to pick up the pieces of the chopstick thing. He shoves them in his pocket. "You need to follow me. Now." His voice sounds sandpapery. His dark eyebrows press into a V shape and he looks grouchier than my mom when she's out of coffee.

I reach down and help Lizzie up. She's grabbing her head and giving me this look like, "OMGWTHBBQ!!11!!"

The small man—he's really small, like smaller than Willy—wheels around, grabs my other arm, and starts pulling me down me street. I dig in my heels.

"I'm sorry," I growl. "We don't have time to be kidnapped right now. We're kind of in the middle of something."

"Willy!" Lizzie shouts, pointing at the line of kids rounding the corner out of sight.

I squint and see her. She has this half smile on her face and she's marching merrily along with the rest of the kids. I dodge the weird little man and run as fast as I can to Willy.

Lizzie and I are shouting her name, but Willy ignores us, marching quickly with the other kids, getting farther and farther away. We catch up and I try to grab her, but she shakes me off with more strength than I thought she had.

"Willy!" I shout again, making another grab for her. "What are you *doing*?"

Lizzie waves her hand in front of the face of the kid in line in front of Willy. "It's like they're hypnotized or something."

Hypnotized. Dude. Is that what was happening with me and Lizzie? I can still feel a bit of the tug toward the blue, blue waves of the ocean. Ahh. The ocean . . .

"BUCK!" Lizzie shoves me in the shoulder. "Snap out of it! She's getting away."

The line of kids is picking up speed.

Lizzie steps away from the marching kids and points. "Look," she says in a strangled voice. The kids are climbing one by one into a Dumpster by the bookstore. What?

A tall kid climbs inside the Dumpster and disappears.

"It's like Mary Poppins's purse," I mutter. Lizzie and I both butt in line and lean over the edge of the Dumpster but it's black inside. And absolutely silent. In fact, everything is silent. Well, everything except for me and Lizzie shrieking all over the place.

Then I notice there's a delivery truck in front of the convenience store across the street and the guy unloading soda bottles is frozen in midstep. Lizzie and I must see the police car in the convenience store parking lot at the same time because she runs over to it, yelling about needing help, but stops short. When I catch up to her I see why. The policeman inside the car is frozen, too. No steam rises from the coffee cup that's halfway to his mouth.

"Buck?" Lizzie's chin quivers. I don't know what to say. I don't know what to do. That's when I look back over my shoulder and see that Willy is almost at the Dumpster.

"Oh no you don't!" I shout, running away from the convenience store and back across the street to her. I grab her arm and pull as hard as I can without hurting her. But now she's leaning into the Dumpster and . . . poof. I feel her arm disappear from my grip.

Disappear from my grip.

Just like that, she's gone.

For a second I think I'm going to throw up. Lizzie is by my side again. We both step back as the endless line continues to move into the Dumpster, the kids disappearing one by one.

"I don't understand," I finally splutter.

"If you're finished running and yelling, I'd like you to come with me." It's the little man again. His arms are crossed over his chest, his jaw tight.

"Are you involved in all this?" I ask, marching over to him. "Where did my sister just go?"

"Macinaw has been kidnapped," the man says, ignoring my question. "I need your help."

I stammer for a minute. "Harold Macinaw? But what about Willy? What about my sister? What about all those kids?" *What about the beach*, my mind tosses at me in a whisper. I put one hand on my forehead to squeeze out the whisper and I throw my other arm out in a helpless gesture at the kids disappearing into the Dumpster.

The small man takes a step closer to me. His scraggly black beard might have grass or sticks or something in it. He looks deranged, and yet his eyes are bright and alert. They look almost familiar somehow. "We need to get you out of here before the effects of my anticurse wear off and you become rehypnotized." He pulls the broken chopstick out of his pocket and stares at it, turning it over and giving it a shake. "I hope we don't get turned inside out," he mutters.

For the first time I notice there's a cut over his left eye and a smear of blood down his hairy arm. His clothes are weird, too.

"Are you wearing . . . bloody hobbit pants?" I whisper, unable to help myself.

The man points a finger at me that turns into a poke in my ribs. "Don't," he says with a look of warning.

"Did you kill a hobbit and steal his pants?" I ask, feeling the craziness of the moment make me a little giddy. "Are you on a journey to fight Smaug?"

"Come with me," he says, pulling at my arm. "Macinaw needs you right now."

"But we don't even *know* Harold Macinaw," Lizzie pipes up.

"Believe me, I know this is . . . unorthodox, but your friend here has been vetted by the highest sources and they say we need him. So here I am, and off we must go." His clutch tightens around my arm. "Getting back is going to be tricky, though, now that you've broken my—"

He lets out a loud piggish squeal as Lizzie hauls off and clonks him over the head with a broken box fan that was lying by the Dumpster. He lets go of my arm so that he can grab his head, and Lizzie takes my hand.

"Come on!" she yells. "Let's get out of here!"

I have never before been in a situation where someone could actually, realistically yell "Come on! Let's get out of here!" It's just like being in a book. But a lot sweatier and scarier.

"Lizzie!" I shout as I stumble-run behind her. "What if he's telling the truth?"

"The truth?!" she shouts over her shoulder. "Are you CRAZY? I know that guy is small, but he is obviously a grown-up, Buck, and he is obviously trying to kidnap you."

I throw a glance behind me and the small man is staring after us, a hand to his bleeding head. Even from a hundred yards away I can see his eyes smoldering. That little dude is not happy with us right now. Not happy at all.

"Uh, Lizzie," I say as we run, "I think we better . . ."

But this time *I* don't have time to finish my sentence because the little man is running full steam at us. He's so fast! And he has his broken chopstick pointed right at us. Uh.

Lizzie grabs my hand. "Buck . . . ," she says. "Maybe we should ru—"

The little man is just feet away now. He flings his chopstick around and around over his head like he's stirring an upside-down pot of soup. For just a second it feels like maybe the invisible soup pot has fallen on me and is crushing my chest. Then there's nothing.

6

There's a cool breeze and then a very loud BANG BANG and when I open my eyes I'm on my knees next to Lizzie in the greenest grass I've ever seen. I catch Lizzie's eye. She opens her mouth to say something, but no words come out.

The sky is a piercing blue, the grass an equally bright green. There's a forest off to the right, but other than that it's all undulating meadow. We are definitely not at home anymore. And we are definitely not at the beach—though the desperate desire to put my toes in warm salt water has faded tremendously. It's now being replaced with panic. Wild-eyed, pants-wetting panic.

The only sounds are the wind rustling the grass, me and

Lizzie hyperventilating, and maybe a bird tweeting in the distance.

I feel a hand on my arm and look down. It's the small man.

"Oh, in the name of Hob's pants, *she* isn't supposed to be here," he says, eyeing Lizzie and then glaring at his broken chopstick thing as if it should come alive and apologize.

"At least we aren't inside out," I sputter, though I kind of feel like I've just been flipped right side in.

"Stay here," he whispers, "I'll be right back." He army-crawls away through the grass.

I look at Lizzie, who can barely shrug. Her mouth is so far open I could see her tail if she had one.

"I'd be offended if I wasn't so freaked out," she breathes.

"Where *are* we?" I whisper-shout after the man, but he's already gone. I drop to my belly and army-crawl after him, ignoring his demand that we stay put. Lizzie is right beside me. She's mostly concealed by the tall grass, but I can see her hair sticking up like a giant, rapidly moving, caramel-colored dandelion.

I don't know where we are or what we're hiding from, but I'm definitely on alert. My heart is thumping, my eyes feel like they're set on Extra Focus, and my ears are tuned to any noise that's not the rustling of tall grass. It's hard to believe that about two minutes ago I was being charged by a tiny man.

I see the man in front of us, still belly-crawling through the grass. I put my finger to my lips and Lizzie makes a face at me. A face that says, "Duh, moron, like I'd stand up and start dancing right now."

Just ahead of the man is a small hole in the ground, and he scampers into it. Lizzie and I approach the opening. It looks big enough to squeeze through. But if we do, I have no idea how we'll get out again.

I tilt my head toward the hole and look at Lizzie. Lizzie blinks once and barely nods. We're like a smooth team of FBI secret service CIA spy soldiers. Or something. I drop myself feetfirst through the hole. It is not a graceful descent. My pajama shirt gets pulled up as I drop down, and mud and dirt smear my chest. I land on the muddy ground with a not very FBI secret service CIA spy soldier "wmmmph-uuugh" kind of grunt. Lizzie lands silently beside me and offers me a hand. She yanks me to my feet and we both do a very poor job of shaking the dirt clumps out of our clothes and hair.

We're half-standing inside a little room that is dark and smells like the almost-black potting soil Mom uses when she plants tomatoes. There's a tunnel winding off ahead of us. That has to be the way the little man went, because I can't see any other exits.

Lizzie starts down the tunnel but stops and turns back when she realizes I'm not right behind her. The tunnel is so low and tight I have to hunch way over to keep from getting my head knocked off. Lizzie has to practically walk on her knees. She reaches for my hand and I'm not embarrassed to take hers. It's dark and close in here, and it's warm and dank. All those descriptive words from bedtime stories that made my heart beat fast when I was little. I trip, then, and feel that the ground is slanting under my feet. We're not just moving farther down the tunnel, we're moving deeper.

After a few minutes of blindly making our way down the tunnel, an eerie glow appears ahead. When my eyes adjust, I see that the tunnel has ended in front of a thick wooden door, with a faintly glowing torch on either side. The top of the door only comes up to the middle of my chest. It's covered in intricately carved designs.

"Eat me," I whisper.

Lizzie whips her head around, her badger teeth bared. "What did you just say?" she says in a shocked tone.

I take a step back and smile. "Eat me," I whisper. "From

Alice in Wonderland. You know, after she falls down the rabbit hole and . . ."

Lizzie waves me off, but I get a half smile out of her.

I really wish I had a mobile phone. Not like it would work underground, but still. I'll have to remember this for the next time Mom and I are arguing about it. "But Mom, what if Lizzie and I get thrown into a bright green meadow and then crawl into a dark dirt tunnel one day? How am I supposed to map my way out—or even see where I'm going?"

"What do we do?" Lizzie whispers, pulling out her phone and shining it around like a flashlight.

"Does the GPS work?" I ask.

"What do you think, goofball?" Lizzie says, shining the light in my face. "I have, like, minus bars down here."

The light from her phone, mixed with the light from the torches, gives the tunnel an eerie TV-ish kind of flicker. I feel a trickle of sweat sliding down my back and into the waistband of my shorts. My glasses slide down my nose because my face is slick with sweat, too. What if the man comes out of the door and sees us here, having disobeyed his order to stay put? What are we even doing here? *Where is this place?*

I swallow a crawling sense of panic and step closer to

the door. It's covered in carvings of battle scenes. In one scene, a bearded man holds a lightning bolt over his head. He's aiming it at a ship on a swirling sea. In another scene, a young man holding what looks like a huge whip stands above a pile of bodies. The bodies are enormous.

"Trolls," I whisper to myself. "And a whip."

"Hmm?" Lizzie says. She peers over my shoulder. "What are you looking at?"

As I run my hands lightly over the door, I can tell the carvings are deep, carefully made. The scene with the guy and the trolls reminds me of *A Tale of Gnomekind* when Custard battles the trolls. I look at Lizzie but stop myself before I say anything. She'll just blink at me like I'm crazy.

But wait.

A Tale of Gnomekind. Book one. Before Custard leaves for battle, he's a student at the Academy.

I look around at the dimness of the tunnel.

No way.

I rub my hands over the carvings again. I look at the iron claws holding the torches.

"Lizzie," I say slowly. I turn my gaze from the door to her face. Our eyes meet. *"Custard tugged at the pack slung over his shoulder. He took a deep breath, the moistness of the air mingling with the hope in his chest. The* carving of the old man in the door was a good likeness of Hob, and Custard was eager to meet the man who would be his teacher; the man who had sent for him; the man who would teach him everything he needed to know to be a man, a mage, a warrior. Custard pushed the door open, entering the Academy."

"Um," Lizzie says. "That's from book one, right? Your voice sounds weird. What's going on?"

I can feel my eyes bugging out of my head as I whip my head around and take in the tunnel one more time. "Everything in this tunnel matches the book, Lizzie. *Everything!*"

"What? *A Tale of Gnomekind?*" Lizzie's eyes go from side to side. "I just see a little door and a lot of dirt."

For a second I feel like I might collapse in on myself. Like, for real. Everything inside me melts. My arms and legs feel loose and dangle-y. My head starts to buzz, my breath comes in short bursts.

"Buck?" Lizzie frowns at me. "Are you okay? Is this a claustrophobic thing? Put your head between your knees."

I spin around, taking in the tunnel again, the torches, the door, the carvings in the door.

"You should probably stop spinning like that," Lizzie says. "You're going to get dizzy and barf. Remember when we went on that field trip to the state capitol?"

Lizzie keeps talking, but her voice blurs into a background drone.

We're at the entrance to the Academy.

The Academy is real.

I move my shaking hands over the blackened iron holding one of the torches. It's almost too hot to touch. I grab handfuls of damp dirt from the wall and let the cool crumbles fall through my fingers to soothe the heat. Then I whip around and grab Lizzie by the shoulders. I start laughing huge, hiccupping snorts.

"Buck! Ew! What's wrong with you?" Lizzie pushes my hands off her shoulders. They've left big muddy handprints on her shirt.

"It's real!" I say between laughs that are threatening to turn into embarrassing tears. "It's all real, Lizzie!"

I can't help myself. I reach out and tug at the iron ring in the center of the door. Nothing. Of course. Then I laugh, because DUH. The secret knock! Everyone knows you can't get into the Academy without the secret knock.

"Buck. Stop. What are you doing?" Lizzie lurches over to me, her face a mask of alarm, but I've already started. Two quick knocks, one bang, two more knocks, a tap on top, a thunk on the bottom, and then a knock on each

side. I hold my breath, tug the iron ring again . . . and the door opens.

I duck under the doorway and the ceiling opens up above me.

Oh, yeah. This is the Academy.

I reach through the doorway and tug Lizzie inside, my face splitting into a huge grin. The entranceway is everything the books said it would be, and yet . . . different. Tunnels lead off in every direction, just as Macinaw described. Most are lined with wood paneling, and a couple of them look like they're made of stone. There's one covered in glittery dark blue and bronze tiles. Everywhere, the floor is wooden and covered in the same kind of carvings as the door. Areas of the carvings are worn down in paths leading to the tunnels.

Macinaw did a good job describing the place, but the *feeling* of the room is different than in the books. It's less happy and shiny, and there's a darkness to everything. The torches on the walls make the shadows harsh and stabby-looking, like animated stalactites and stalagmites. It's not like how I imagined it at all, really. I feel like I can smell the blood from the battles depicted on the floor. I'm glad Willy isn't here with me. She'd need two pocketfuls of her antiworrying Silly Putty for this.

Even so, the place is amazing. And it's real. I kneel down and rub my hand over the carvings on the floor. Lizzie kneels next to me, her mouth hanging slightly open. She blinks at me, really fast, and I blink back. Her hand snakes out and pinches me on the arm.

"Ow!" I whisper, rubbing the red spot.

"Just making sure we're not dreaming this," she whispers back. "And getting you back for messing up my shirt."

I want to run around the room and laugh and spin in circles like whatsherface in *The Sound of Music*, or yell like Bastian does when he rides the luckdragon for the first time. But I'm trying to keep cool. Seeing as how we're still supposed to be crouched down in a meadow waiting for the little man to return, shouting and weeping and spinning in circles is probably a bad idea. But trust me, I'm shouting and weeping and spinning in circles on the inside.

I stand up and wipe my sweaty hands on my shorts. An empty desk sits directly in front of us. From the books, I know that Sara, the goblin receptionist, is supposed to be there. Plus, I can see a small steaming mug next to an open catalogue of goblin skin-care products. I run over to the catalogue and hold it up for Lizzie to see. It's open to a page that says, *For all your skin slickening needs.*

There's a picture of a lady goblin slathering some kind of goo onto her face.

"This is bananas, Buck," Lizzie whispers through her hands, which are clutching at her mouth like she's just seen a three-headed snake. "Ba. Nan. Ahs."

"It's real, it's real, it's real" is the only thing going through my head as I carefully put the catalogue down and gaze back out at the tunnels.

I'm amazed there's no one around. In the books, *the main hall is always bustling with gnomes of all kinds, moving here and there, busy about their days*. But right now it's totally deserted. Good for us, but weird.

I point down one of the halls and motion for Lizzie to follow me. She shakes her head. "If this really is the Academy," she whispers fiercely, "we could be killed for being in here. Remember chapter five? In book two?"

I'm impressed she knows her chapters this well. Lizzie is a huge Triumphant Gnome Syndicate fan like I am, but she's not quite as obsessive. No one is. I mean, can *you* tell me how much Harold Macinaw weighed when he was born? Do you know what page of book one has a secret reference to his birth weight? Yeah, well, I do.

Lizzie has a pretty good point, though. The gnomes are not really into having visitors. Those poor brownies in chapter five had no idea what was coming. They were just lost and looking for directions and then . . . I shiver. But that was a book, and this is real life. We're *inside* the *actual* Academy. No one's going to hurt us. Why would they? They probably don't even think *we* exist! I have to stop for a minute to let that sink in.

"It'll be fine," I say, ignoring every time I've yelled at someone who has said that exact same thing in a book. "Come on." I tug on her hand until she's following me down one of the wood-paneled tunnels. As we make our way down, the walls of the tunnel become increasingly crowded with small round doors.

"Must be the living quarters," I whisper.

One of the doors bursts open, the little man flings himself at us, and before we can protest, he's shoved us through the door and into a tiny room.

"What part of 'wait for me' did you not understand?" he growls, locking the door behind him. "I specifically said I'd be back, and I specifically did NOT invite you down here— especially *her*. I thought you were familiar with the laws of Flipside? Don't you know what can happen if you're dis- covered here?"

Lizzie crosses her arms over her chest and juts out her hip, ready to launch into him for being rude, but I cut her off. "You can't just bring us to THE REAL FLIPSIDE and then expect us to sit still and not look around!" I seriously feel like I might explode with excitement. "Can you introduce us to Sara? I've always imagined what goblins would be like in real life, but getting the chance to—"

The man reaches up and puts his small, dirty hand on my mouth. He gives me a look that would wither a tree. He brings a finger to his mouth in a slow exaggerated way to tell me to shush. Then he takes that same finger and points to the door he closed behind us. "Be quiet, human," he seethes. "If anyone sees you, they will take you prisoner. You will be given a Trial of Epic Importance and found guilty of spying. Then they will kill you. After that, they will kill me."

Lizzie's eyes go wide. "Trials of Epic Importance are *real*?!"

The man puckers his face into a scowl. "Yes. Real."

"Whoa," I say. My arms prickle with goose bumps. "But don't you mean we'll be found guilty of spying and then banished? Or sentenced to kitchen labor? Gnomes don't believe in killing as a punishment. *A kind and gentle race of creatures, gnomes work to keep the peace and*—"

The man grunts and cuts me off. "I mean you'll be

sentenced to being dropped into a pit filled with acid vipers, and I will, too."

Acid vipers?! That's not in any of the books. I have so many questions. Like, so, so many questions. I don't even know where to start. How did we get here? Are all the books true? Is Custard in a room down the hall? Am I in the same building as Custard?! No, that couldn't be right, because he was off at war in *Gnome-a-geddon*. But it doesn't look like there's a war going on. I mean, from the ten minutes I've been in a meadow and now here. Also, if I'm here, why does it matter if Lizzie's here, too? Also, also, where the heck is Willy? And Macinaw is supposed to be kidnapped? I'm afraid my head is going to literally fly off my shoulders and explode in the air like those whirligig fireworks that chase Dad down the street when he lights them.

Through the dim light of a lamp, I can see that the room is small and round. No corners. No windows. There's a small, unmade bed, a table covered in bits of leather and brass doodads, clothes everywhere, and a poster of Lady Gaga.

I point to the poster and before I can say anything, the man mutters, "Banished. Half-gnome. That poster is allowed! Sort of."

I nod, not knowing how to respond.

He points to the messy bed. His bed, I guess? "Sit."

Lizzie and I do what he says even though sitting on some stranger's messy bed seems like yet another thing I would yell at someone in a book for doing. I mean, gross.

"Clearly, you both need a lesson on following directions." The man's dark eyes flash.

"Gnomes are real!" I blurt out. "Holy crap!"

"Indeed," he says with a sigh. "I was going to break it to you Topside, but then you snapped my weapon in half and threw my entire plan out of whack." He takes a deep breath. "It was *incredibly* stupid of you to follow me into the Academy. It's very, very unsafe for you in here." He runs his hands over his face, ending with a little tug of his beard. "I thought you were an expert on the books, Buck." He shakes his head. "Anyway, I need you both to listen very carefully." He takes two steps closer to us. I can smell the dirt and sweat on him.

"My name is Smith. You are going to have to do everything I say, exactly when I say it, for us to get out of here alive. Do you understand me?"

I swallow and yank my hand off the bedspread when I realize it's been resting on a pair of tiny underpants.

"A gnome has gone missing. You're acquainted with him? Harold Macinaw?"

"H-Harold Macinaw is a gnome?" I stammer.

"Of course, of course," Smith says impatiently. "Did you think he was just a short man interested in telling stories?"

Lizzie and I look at each other.

"Actually, yeah, that *is* what we thought," I say.

"Wrong," Smith says, opening a jar and dabbing some cream on one of his scratches. "He's a gnome who was banished Topside years and years ago. And now someone has taken him. We were told that you"—Smith points at me—"would be helpful in our search to find him."

"Me?" I say. "Who told you that?"

"Doesn't matter," Smith says. "What matters is that we're already behind schedule. We need to get out of here, find the Troll Vanquishing Mace, and then find Macinaw." He turns his laser stare to Lizzie and waves his hand at her. "I need to know whether this girl is going to be a help or a hindrance to our cause. She wasn't part of my instructions. . . ." He trails off and looks her up and down with squinting eyes. "We do not need anything or anyone to slow us down."

"Hey!" Lizzie protests. "Of course I'm helpful."

"She does have a cell phone," I say, and Lizzie elbows me in the ribs.

Smith walks two steps over to a dark wood basin with a brass interior. He looks over his shoulder at us. Then, as he washes his face, he mumbles to himself, "I can't believe this is what the prophecy meant."

"Wait. What? Prophecy?" Lizzie looks from Smith to me and back to Smith again.

I snort out a laugh. *"Prophecy?* You can't be serious. There aren't prophecies Flipside. Macinaw would never put anything like that into his books. It's lazy writing. He doesn't even use mystics or fortune-tellers."

Smith stuffs supplies into a bag and opens his mouth to say something. There's a soft knock on the door. He closes his mouth, then opens it again, his voice quiet and fierce. "You need to hide. Right now."

Hide?

Lizzie and I look around the room. Everything is a third the size of the furniture in my house. I don't see a closet door or bathroom door anywhere. But then I remember the description of the Academy rooms in book one. Many of the rooms have a trapdoor under the bed. It's how the student gnomes secretly tunnel their way out to solve mysteries and save the less fortunate. I lift up the bed, and sure enough, there's a wooden door in the floor. Smith comes over and takes the edge of the bed from me so I can kick open the latch on the wooden door. Lizzie and I climb quickly down into the hole. The trapdoor shuts over us, plunging us into complete darkness. I hear the bed land on top of the wood above us and a swirl of claustrophobia crawls up my throat.

There are muffled footsteps and a door slamming. Then nothing.

Awesome.

7

The trapdoor creaks open and Lizzie and I shield our eyes. The dim light seems like an explosion after being in the pitch black.

"Listen," Smith says, looking down on us and slinging his bag over his shoulder. "We have about three minutes to get out of here. Sara is doing all she can to keep everyone occupied so I can get cleaned up and gather some supplies. The Syndicate has . . . well, the Syndicate has interpreted the prophecy in a different way." He shakes his head and makes a disgruntled noise. "Anyway, Sara's going to have to get back to her desk soon, so we have to get out of here."

"Is that who was at the door?" Lizzie asks. She

turns to me and grins. "Sara is real! I love Sara!"

Smith frowns. "Why would you love Sara? She was coming back from the bathroom when she saw you two come in the entrance. Nice stealthy work there." He rolls his eyes. "I had to bribe her with two bags of goblin gold to keep her mouth shut and watch the hallway. You know how long I've been saving that up?" He makes another grouchy noise and says, "Let's go."

I put a hand on his arm. All the excitement and craziness of the situation has stopped making me dizzy, and now it's making me nauseous. I mean, I love Harold Macinaw and everything, but I love Willy more. I can't be getting myself involved in some stupid prophecy plot when Willy is here lost somewhere. I need to be searching for her. The more I think about it, the more panicked I feel. If I'm freaking out this much, Willy is probably legit bonkers by now.

"I can't go with you on some crazy search for the Troll Vanquishing Mace, Smith. For one thing, it's fictional. Or at least, this morning it was fictional. For another thing, if it's not fictional then it's *lost to the sands of time, a weapon of danger better suited to myth than reality.* I can't be going on some wild quest while Willy is lost. I have to find her. Once she's safe I can totally help you, though."

"You don't understand," Smith says. He's taking deep breaths, obviously trying to control his growing impatience. "It has to be *you* who finds the mace. And it has to be *you* who wields the mace to save Macinaw. It's been foreseen in the unicorn's prophecy. I can't change any of that. It *has* to be you."

"Wait, wait . . . unicorn?!" Lizzie and I go bug-eyed. There are no unicorns in the books!

"So this"—Lizzie pauses, closes her eyes, and then slowly opens them—"*unicorn* said Buck's name?" She scrunches up her nose. "It yelled out *Buck Rogers, he of irritating parents who named him after a TV show, has to be the guy who lops off the head of the evil troll holding Harold Macinaw hostage*? Little dude, that is crazy. I don't believe it."

"Never call me *little dude*," Smith growls. "And no, it did not say his name specifically, but it said enough for me to know."

"But how?" Lizzie presses. "You have a list of every kid in the world and whether or not they read Macinaw's books?"

Smith grinds his teeth, his jaw set. "Your questions are all irrelevant—what matters now is finding the mace and saving Macinaw."

I finally pipe up, after having watched their conversation like a tennis match. "We can spend days hunting for that thing, Smith. Months . . . years . . . it won't matter if we find it because only a Halfling can wield it. It says so right in the Scrolls of Gnomekind. *Only he who is part of gnome and part of newer kind can be the master of the mace.*" I pull my *extra* extra copy of *A Tale of Gnomekind* from my back pocket (my second copy because Willy keeps stealing my first copy). I flip through the pages to find the passage I'm looking for and then jam my finger at the tiny words. "See? Halfling." My lips purse in triumph. "Are you part human? No. Am I part gnome? No."

Smith just stares at me like I have something slithering out of my nose. He makes a show of rolling his eyes.

"Buck." Lizzie's whole face seems to be expanding. Her eyes widening, her mouth falling open . . .

I hold up the book and point at the words a couple more times as if that will make everyone suddenly pay attention. "Right here," I say. "Proof." I tap once more. "Must be a Halfling, therefore, waste of our time. Hey! Maybe Lady Gaga is the answer to your prophecy!" I nod, trying to get Smith to nod with me. "Or maybe Lizzie is the Halfling, she's got that whole multiracial thing going on." Lizzie hauls off and punches me in the shoulder.

"Ow!" I rub the throbbing spot. "Was that insensitive of me? I just meant . . . you know . . ."

Lizzie blows air out of her mouth and shakes her head.

Smith chews his bottom lip and looks at Lizzie. Lizzie looks back at him as if daring him to say something. Then she takes a deep breath, closes her eyes, and opens them.

"Buck," she says again. "Think about it."

Smith marches past us and looks through the peephole in his door.

"You *really* want us to go on this crazy quest?" I shout after him. I wave the book. "Why are you ignoring this?"

"BUCK! JEEZ!" Lizzie grabs me by the shoulders and gives me a shake. "He's trying to tell you *you* are a Halfling! DUH!"

My body goes limp as Lizzie flops me back and forth. The hand that holds the book drops to my side. Everything seems to go fuzzy around the edges, and then I snap out of it. Ridiculous. "You're just as crazy as he is," I say, wrenching out of Lizzie's grip. "There's no way I'm a Halfling. There are pictures of me being born. Like, a disgusting video and everything. If my mom or dad was a gnome, don't you think I'd know that?" I flip through the book again, as if there might be some kind of answer in it to the question of my lineage. "There's no way Mom is a gnome," I say.

"And your dad is like seven feet tall," Lizzie says. "True. Hmm."

Smith turns around, his eyes burning. "Just follow me. If you hear the prophecy for yourself, will you help me? Will you find Macinaw and save the gnomes?"

"If I hear this stupid prophecy and it's all, *Buck Rogers, you're our only hope*, I'll for sure think about it, because whoa. BUT! I'm going to find my sister first. Then Macinaw."

"Absolutely," Smith says, but he's not looking at me when he talks, and I bet a thousand percent that his fingers are crossed behind his back.

Smith ducks his head out the doorway and makes sure no one is out there, and we follow him into the hall. He produces a brand-new chopstick thingy and taps the door to his room three times. I notice that it has a little piece of leather or something hanging from its tip.

"What is that little thing?" I ask, grasping at something forming in my brain. "Is it your . . . whip?"

Lizzie gasps.

"You're *Custard*, aren't you? Teenage Gnome of the West?!" My mouth falls open.

Smith reaches up and grabs me by the shirt, yanking me down to eye level. "Never call me that. *Never*." His voice is low and angry. "My name is Smith. It's not Custard, never has been Custard. I don't wear a pointy hat, and I'm not a noble hero. So can that Custard garbage right now."

I put my hands up. "Okay, okay."

"Follow me. Quietly." We do as he says, but my mind isn't very quiet at all.

The unicorn is not real. So that's a bummer. It's some kind of mechanized robot thing. In the glow from a glass orb at the back of the cavern, I can see the joints and screws that make its mouth move. It reminds me of the giant Rudolph head at the mall around Christmastime. There's this box that's big, like the size of a man standing on another man's shoulders, and way up high is an opening where Rudolph's big, fake head pokes out. There is some poor person crammed in the lower part of the box talking into a microphone and somehow making the head move around. *You in the red dress, do you think Santa has you on the nice list? Hey, kid in the hat, stop throwing ice cream at my stable.* Rudolph is there to keep the kids entertained while they wait in an epic line to see Santa. Clearly, this fake unicorn is here to keep gnomes entertained while they wait for the trolls to all get abducted by aliens or something.

"Do you have to put a quarter in it to make it work?" I walk closer and see that the joints and screws are all old and rusty. The eyes are pieces of glass set in the painted metal. Kind of like marbles, I guess, but instead of being pretty and glossy they're solid yellow and milky and super-creepy. This thing looks like someone ripped it off a merry-go-round, left it in a backyard for a million years, and then made a not-so-great effort at cleaning off all the dirt and grass and whatnot.

Smith gives me a sour look and goes to the side of the unicorn, where a rusty crank sticks out from its flank. He gives it three solid turns. I can tell the last turn is difficult because Smith grunts just a little bit, though his expression is all, "Look how strong I am, turning this unicorn flank crank like it's nothing."

"I haven't read the books as obsessively as you have, Buck, but I don't remember anything about talking robot unicorns." Lizzie has one hand on her hip and she looks like she wants to burst out laughing at any second.

"That is because talking robot unicorns are almost as stupid as prophecies."

"Shut your mouths, both of you," Smith growls. His words are low and tight and angry. "This is a sacred space and I'm breaking ancient law by even allowing you to accompany me here. There are no unicorns in your precious books because even Harold Macinaw himself wasn't allowed in this room. Show some respect before I grab you both by your hair and fling you back Topside where you belong."

There is a terribly loud sound of metal screeching on metal, and we all grab our ears. Smith yells, "Step back!" Lizzie and I have already retreated almost as far as the doorway. How are we supposed to be here in secret with this kind of noise?

The fake unicorn's fake mouth opens, like Zoltar's in the movie *Big*. It closes. Then opens again. Then closes. The yellow eyes begin to glow as the mouth opens one more time, but more slowly.

If a busted, rusted washing machine could talk, it would sound prettier than the unicorn's scratched metallic voice. Its mouth hangs open, not even trying to move as if talking for real. The words scrape from the mouth and into our ears in a way that almost hurts.

"*The world is cracked open. With a mighty swing from unpracticed arms, the secret-knowing Halfling* wields the mace. The Halfling restores balance as the bruising fates bring about a new day, and what's lost is found again, the world forever changed."

The mouth creaks shut, the glow goes out of the eyes, and the unicorn is once again still.

Smith is breathing hard, eyes wide. His hand pulls down over his face, wiping off sweat. His expression is hard to read but his eyes seem to offer a clue to how he's feeling. Maybe surprised. Maybe scared.

"*That's* the prophecy?" I wrinkle my nose. "It's so boring. And it doesn't even really say anything. This is why prophecies are so lame. You know, Macinaw would never use a prophecy in one of his books. He's a better writer than that."

"This is real life, Buck. I can't help it if you don't find it believable." The light from the orb is dimming, throwing long shadows everywhere. The creep factor of the cavern has gone up by about fifty percent in the past two minutes.

"Can we get out of here now?" I ask.

"Scared of a—what did you call it? Talking robot unicorn?" Smith's half smile doesn't reach his eyes.

"No," I say. "it's just that . . ."

"Yes," Lizzie answers for me. "The talking robot unicorn is super-creepy, Smith. Can we leave now?"

But before we can do anything, we all hear marching footsteps coming down the tunnel outside the cavern. Smith ducks his head out the doorway, ducks quickly back into the cavern with us, and takes out the tiny whip.

"Don't make a sound. And don't move unless I tell you to move. When I tell you to move, don't ask questions, just do as I say." His whisper is fierce. Smith cracks the whip and somewhere farther down the tunnel a couple of rocks clack together as they fall.

"Up there!" a voice yells, and three gnomes run past the opening to the cavern without even looking in.

"That's a pretty magical whip," I whisper.

"It's not a whip," Smith says. "Now come on." He bolts out the doorway and runs in the opposite direction from the gnomes who just ran past. Lizzie and I are right behind him.

We're almost to the end of the tunnel when someone yells, "Hey! Up there! Yoomans! Get them!" and I have to give myself a quick talking-to about how sixth graders can be brave enough to not faint or barf or faint AND barf at the first sign of danger. (Even when they're about to be caught and killed by gnomes who were up to this point thought to be fairly harmless adventurers. And also fictional.)

Three gnomes are running at top speed through the tunnel, toward us. It's pretty dark but I can tell they aren't wearing red pointy hats like they would be in the book. And they aren't smiling and joking like they would be in the book. As they get closer I can see their faces are flushed, their eyes narrowed. One of the gnomes raises a weapon I've never seen before. Kind of like a slingshot gun.

"Go! Go! Go!" Smith yells, all pretense of whispering gone.

Loud THUNKs and BAMs explode in the dirt walls around us.

"What are they shooting?" I yell. "Will it kill us?" In the books, only certain gnomes have very specialized weapons, like Custard's whip or Maori's fishhook. There are no slingshot gun things.

"Maybe!" Smith yells. "Or they could be stunners, so that we can be more easily captured and taken prisoner. Either way, let's not find out!"

There's a ladder up ahead, and Lizzie leaps on it. I'm right behind her and Smith is pushing at my butt, yelling, "Get a move on!"

"I'm moving, I'm moving," I say.

There's an explosion of dirt above my head and Lizzie gives a little squeak. Then she's scrambling up and off the top of the ladder, through a hole in the ceiling of the tunnel. I'm right behind her. The hole is covered in clumps of damp, black dirt. We push our way through like we're being born up through the ground, or maybe like we're zombies climbing out of a grave. We get through the last of the dirt and the sunshine is blinding.

Smith clambers up behind us and hollers, "Follow me!" My eyes are watering furiously from the sunlight. I can only open them a tiny crack. I take off my filthy glasses and wipe my eyes and then put them back on again. Totally didn't help at all. I think we're back in the meadow. Smith darts around my side and I chase after him, trying not to lose sight of him, even though tears are streaming down my face from the sudden brightness. If light could scream, the afternoon would be yelling right in my face.

"Are you okay?" I shout to Lizzie. Her blurry figure is scrambling beside me. There's dirt in her hair and smeared on her face. She doesn't say anything, but she doesn't look hurt.

"There they are!" a voice yells behind us. I turn and see the three gnomes climbing out of the hole. Uh-oh.

"Come on," Smith says. He whirls around toward the forest and we chase after him.

"We can hide in the forest. Katya will help," he says as he runs. "Well, maybe."

Lizzie has slowed down, so I grab her arm and drag her with me. Something's not right. She's too quiet. Her eyes are too wide.

"Did you get hit?" I ask her as we run.

She doesn't answer.

"Who's Katya?" I call to Smith. He waves his arms to shush me.

We're in the forest now. The green surrounding us has gone from a brilliant grassy shimmer to a deep velvet gloss. The scent of pine needles is so strong, I can almost taste it.

Smith stops and Lizzie and I crash into him. "Over here," he whispers, and we run behind a huge boulder. It seems like the most obvious hiding place ever, but a minute later the three gnomes run right past us.

"So who's—?" I whisper, and then a sheen of bright white crashes over my field of vision. I hear something that sounds like metal twisting and think it might be the sound of my head popping off my body.

The deep green fades to black.

"This is Katya," Smith says as my eyes fight against opening. "An impetuous gnome who loves complicating situations even more than they're already complicated." My hand goes to my head. Still attached. Whew. It hurts, though—man, it hurts! A drip of sticky wetness tickles the side of my face.

I crack open an eye and see a dirty girl standing over me. Or maybe a lady. I don't know. Where are my glasses? I frantically pat the leaves and sticks around my head until my hand snags on my wire-frames. I put my glasses on. Mom gripes a lot about how much they cost, but hooray for composite lenses that don't smash unless you run over them with a truck.

The lady doesn't seem that old, but she's definitely older than me. She's small, like Smith, which isn't a surprise. Her nose turns up like all gnomes' noses do. Her blond hair is dirty, full of leaves and twigs, and she's wearing the same kind of burlap pants as Smith, but with a pair of leather-looking suspenders crossed over her chest in an X. There are all kinds of things hanging off the X. Little axes, vials, a slingshot. She's holding a small wooden club that I'm pretty sure exactly matches a certain dent in my head.

I try to sit up and just as the pain is telling me that's a terrible idea, I notice Katya has a heavy foot on my chest. She's holding Lizzie by the waistband of her pants with her other hand.

"Why were you shouting my name, troll?" She sneers down at me.

"I'm not a troll," I whisper, wincing at the noise of her voice. "My name is Buck. I'm—"

"He's very important," Smith says, interrupting me, "which is why I would like him to continue to *stay alive*, please, Katya. Put the club down."

I'd proudly puff out my chest if it didn't have a foot on it.

Katya lowers the club a millimeter.

"Now tell me, what is this, Katya?" Smith says, his *eyes* flashing.

"I've brained a yooman and captured another one," Katya says, smiling down at me. Her teeth are dirty, too. "These two should earn me a nice bounty from the goblins."

"I'm not talking about them," Smith says. Is he sneering or smiling? The world spins. "I'm talking about this." He waves his arms around. "You really do live in the forest now? All alone? Like some hermit?"

Katya's eyes narrow. "I don't answer to you, Sheriff," she snarls. "Not anymore. Yes, I'm on my own. It's better this way. Easier." Smith makes to move closer, to look at my head, but she puts a hand out and stops him. He bats it away. Why hasn't Lizzie asked if I'm okay? Why isn't she trying to drop-kick this mean gnome across the forest? Katya only has her by her waistband. She should've turned around and busted free by now. I try to hiss Lizzie's name, but Katya presses her boot deeper into my chest.

"What are you doing in my forest, anyway, Sheriff?" Katya asks Smith.

"We're looking for Macinaw," Smith says. His hands are clenching into fists. "I thought maybe you could help us, you crazy troll. I wasn't expecting to have to fight you to the death." He eyes her club, which she finally lowers all the way to her side. "And this isn't *your* forest."

Katya looks genuinely surprised. "Yoomans? *Macinaw*

lost? Are you saying the prophecy is finally coming true?"

I would laugh if I didn't have a foot on my chest. Again with the prophecy talk. A lot of people seem to know about this thing for it to be such a secret.

Katya lets go of Lizzie and takes her foot off my chest so she can walk closer to Smith. "I would as soon cut off my hands as help that toad Macinaw. Prophecy or not." She spits on the ground.

There is not this much spitting in the books.

With great effort, I roll over and grab at Lizzie's dirty shoe. She's just standing there gazing up at the trees. She still doesn't look at me, even as I pinch her ankle and hiss her name.

"Regardless of how you feel about Macinaw, this boy is my responsibility," Smith says, as much in Katya's face as she was in his. "When everything turns to troll scat you need to make sure you truly are on our side. I wouldn't want to think about what kinds of punishment the Syndicate would create just for you."

Katya grabs Smith's fingers like she's going to rip them off. His lips spread into some kind of shape that I think means he's trying to show her that it doesn't hurt, even though it really, really does. "I. Am. Not. On. Your. Side." She gives his fingers a squeeze and his grimace deepens.

"I'm not on anyone's side, mind you. I'm on *my* side. Katya's side. Like I should have been the whole time." She raises a hand, and with a flick of her wrist a wind rises and smashes Smith back against a tree trunk. He clambers to his feet and shakes sticks from his hair. Then he grabs the whip from his pocket and points it at Katya's face. She cackles and raises her other hand.

"Okay, okay," I say, pushing myself into a sitting position and fighting the swirling nausea from the pain in my head. "This is a charming display of mutual hatred, but I would like to hit the pause button for a moment so you can turn your attention to this. . . ." I point to Lizzie. She's now sitting next to me, scooping dirt into piles and gently licking leaves. "What's the matter with her?"

They both look at Lizzie. Smith opens his mouth to say something but then shuts it again. Katya kneels next to Lizzie and roughly grabs her face. Lizzie doesn't even seem to notice.

"Mindbombs," Katya says. She turns to me. "You were chased here, yes?"

I nod.

She reaches up to her left shoulder and pulls what looks like a clod of dirt off her suspenders. "Were they shooting these things at you?"

"I—I'm not sure," I say. "Could be. They were shooting *something*."

Katya looks at Smith.

"We were running pretty fast," he says. "Could have been mindbombs, stunners, soulstinkers, any number of things."

Soulstinkers? The heck?

Katya turns Lizzie's head to one side and then to the other. "I'm going with mindbomb." She releases Lizzie's chin and wipes her hands on her pants.

"What is your name, girl?" she asks.

Lizzie says nothing. She just stares off into the distance

"How old are you?"

Lizzie still doesn't say anything. I think she might be starting to drool.

"Looks like you got yourselves a walking turnip," Katya says.

"What?!" I try to stand, but my head bursts into stars and flames and it feels like Troll Vanquishing Maces are smashing into my eyes. Man, Katya really walloped me good.

"Well, that's just great," Smith says, throwing his arms into the air. "I already didn't need the extra baggage, and now the extra baggage can't even think straight?!"

First Willy goes missing and now Lizzie is a turnip? I want to argue with him, to shout and fight and figure out a plan, but the pain is so terrible, I can only sit on the ground and moan.

"I think I need a doctor," I say, gagging. "And, obviously, so does Lizzie."

Smith sighs. "Are you kidding me, Buck? We don't have time for that. And I don't have the gold to bribe someone to look at you. Man up."

"Man up?!" I shout, and then wince, choking down bile. "Your stupid girlfriend bashed in my brains so she could sell me to the goblins!"

"She's not my girlfriend," Smith says at the same time Katya says, "He's not my boyfriend."

"She was once, though, wasn't she?" I croak. "Canopy, right? In the books? You're Canopy DaSilva, Custard's one and only love. She got mad at the Syndicate after they gave her the crappy power of manipulating wind." Katya's face flushes. "Sorry," I say. "I mean the *interesting* and *important* ability to blow the wind around." I wave my arms around and attempt a smile, but Katya lunges at me and I flinch. "Canopy ran away to live in the Darkest Forest," I continue. "She—" I look over at Lizzie. This is when she would normally start blinking at me to tell me I was saying too much and driving everyone crazy. She's just sitting there, though, staring up at the tops of the trees again. "It's all in book two," I say. "*Little Big Gnome*?" My voice slides out like air slipping out of a deflating balloon. I can feel my heartbeat in my eyes.

"Fan of those nasty books, huh, troll?" Katya says, coming closer to me.

"I. Am. Not. A. Troll," I say between clenched teeth.

"She doesn't really think you're a troll, you half-wit. She's swearing at you."

I give Smith Lizzie's best badger face. "Huh?"

"What," he says, with a laugh, "Macinaw didn't write any gnome swearing into his precious little books?"

"The goblins are never going to give me any gold for a stuttering moron and his turnip," Katya says to herself, shaking her head. She puts her hand out to help me to my feet. "I guess if the prophecy is coming true we should probably keep you alive." Her voice is strangled and her eyes dart from my face to my feet. "As much as I would enjoy parading my yooman catch from town to town and taking gold from the highest bidder, well . . . down the path about four hundred paces is a small hut. A healer. Tell him I sent you. Have him look at the girl, too. Maybe there's something he can do. After that, get out of my forest."

"It's *not* your forest." Smith grimaces.

Katya shakes her head. "Just get out of my sight, goblin. And take your trolls with you." She points down a barely marked path. "Four hundred paces." She moves her hand like a puppet mouth. *"Katya sent me. Please don't shoot."*

"D-don't shoot?" I stammer. Smith grabs my arm and I pull Lizzie to her feet. We walk down the path and I feel like someone should be off to the side singing, *"We welcome you to munchkin land, fa la la la la la la la la la."* Only in a slow-motion version that's even creepier than the original.

I wouldn't call this a hut. I'd call it a pile of filthy leaves.

"Sooo . . . ," I say. "Do we knock, or—?"

Smith drops to his hands and knees and crawls down into the leaves. A minute or two later his head pops up out of the leaves and he says, "Get down here. He'll help us, but he's not thrilled about it."

By this time, the excitement of crawling through grass and dirt and holes is starting to wear off. I push Lizzie through the dirty leaves and partially into the hole. When I know Smith has her, I stick my feet in to follow.

I feel two hands grip my legs from either side. Instead of yanking me into the hole, they gently pull me down. As my eyes adjust to the dimness, I see that the hand on the right comes from Smith and the hand on the left comes from some gnarled creature that looks like a cross between a sweet potato and a possum.

"Whoa!" I stumble out of their grasp and back away, hitting a dirt wall behind me. We're in a small, cluttered room. There are some tiny chairs up against the wall beside me, and a bunch of shelves cover the other walls. The shelves are full of zillions of jars and vials. Lizzie is in a chair next to where I'm standing, watching with no expression. She's starting to remind me of Fake Lizzie, and that's freaking me out more than my head wound.

The potato-looking possum thing takes a step toward me. He's a little bit shorter than Smith, but only by an inch or so. He tries to sticks his long snout in my face but manages, instead, to stare at me from just above my belly button.

"Who you are? Why help you ask me for?" he snarls, showing two rows of sharp yellow teeth. "Not very smart, to go get beat about the head in the forest, huh? Do you think?"

"What?" I say. My head is pounding. "Katya said you . . . *aaaarfff.*" I lean forward and barf all over the creature's feet. "Sorry," I say, wiping my mouth with the back of my hand.

"You do no more talking, yes?" the creature says, grabbing my arm and leading me to a chair that's at least one size too small for me and filled with dried-up roots and piles of things that look suspiciously like poop. He grabs Smith's hand and uses it to clear off the seat.

"Hey!" Smith protests.

The creature sits me down and my bottom just barely squishes in. The potato-possum pinches my eyelids, sniffs my earholes, looks under my arms, and puts clawed fingers into my hair and picks around like they do at school when they're looking for lice.

"You'll live," he mutters.

I look at Smith and Smith shrugs like, "I don't know, just be cool."

The creature putters over to a table covered in leaves and paper and glass vials and hunks of potentially rotten meat. He picks up a glass beaker and spits into it; then he uses his filthy shirt to wipe it "clean."

"I'm gonna barf again," I say, but Smith gives me A Look That Stops Barf.

The creature grabs handfuls of this and that off the table, including a handful of the poop-looking stuff. He mixes it up with a stick and then snaps his fingers, creating a small flame out of one of his claws.

"Whoa," I say.

The creature heats the bottom of the beaker until the goop inside has turned into a steaming pile of sludge; then he slides the beaker into a metal sleeve with a handle on it and hands it to me, like it's a cup of coffee.

"Drink," he says. "All of it. Then fine you be."

"I don't want to drink this," I say to Smith. "Like, for real. I'll take my chances with the concussion."

"DRINK!" the creature shouts, his sweet-potato face going ruby red. "YOU DRINKS IT NOW!"

"I'd drink it," Smith says, trying not to smile.

I shoot him a deathly stare and bring the beaker to my lips. The smell is nothing I can describe. Just—the worst of all things you could ever imagine all mixed up together. We're talking baby diapers and puke and roadkill—everything.

"Fast you drink it," the creature says, his voice a bit softer now. "Fast, fast."

I take a deep breath and toss back the entire contents of the beaker. I try to swallow, but it's too thick, so I have to chew a couple of times.

Oh my God. It is so terrible.

A squeak snorts out of Smith's nose as he tries to stifle a laugh.

I choke the poop smoothie down and concentrate on not barfing it back up.

"Good. Good," the creature says, taking the beaker from me. "Now you stay living and breathing. Good, yes?"

I nod, unable to speak. My throat has been scorched to death by a roadkill milk shake.

"Time to stew it in your guts," he says. "Now what problems this lass having?" He turns to Lizzie.

"Mindbomb," Smith says. "At least we think so."

The creature shakes his head. "Mindbombs is not so easily reversible. They bad news all day long."

"You have to help her," I say. "She's my . . . she's my Lizzie."

The creature gives her the same kind of examination he gave me but spends extra time looking in her eyes. He's so still for so long, I wonder if he's somehow been hypnotized. Then he quickly frisks her and pulls her mobile phone from her pocket. It's dented and filthy. The creature jumps up and down and claps, making me and Smith jump, too.

"I think it's just a partial hit," he says, his nose twitching in excitement. "Look at this thing with its dents and whatnots. I think most of the blow it took. I think maybe I can help this girl!" He hands me the filthy, broken phone and toddles over to a table and sorts through piles of moss and leaves, cracking things into a small paper bag.

I can't wait to tell Mom that Lizzie's cell phone saved her life. Reasons for Buck to get a phone: LOTS. Reasons for Mom to deny Buck this necessity: FEWER AND FEWER.

When the creature's done dropping things into the paper bag, he gives the bag a couple of whacks with a wooden hammer, then shakes it up and pours the dust into his hand. He walks back over to Lizzie.

"Girlie-o, hello?" He waggles his fingers and she turns to blankly stare at him. He blows the whole poof of dust into her face and she coughs and sputters and waves her arms, accidentally smacking him in the head. He falls to the ground, right by my feet. By the time he stands up, she's out of it again.

"Hmm. She not perfect," the yam-faced man says, rubbing at his backside. "I cannot be fixing all of the troubles the mindbombs cause. But there's a tricky trick I could give a go at. Could maybe fix her up. Or maybe kill her dead." He shrugs. "Just need spicy tree frings and some rootflop and we can test it out."

Lizzie's eyes suddenly go wide. She lets out a shriek, and the creature blows something else in her face, which makes her eyes roll back in her head. She snores lightly.

"I don't know about any experimental treatments," I say. "That sounds too—"

"Too late!" The ugly creature cackles and wipes his hands on his shirt. "We give her five of the minutes. She be dead, or she be fixed. Ta-da!"

I feel suddenly dizzy as I look at Lizzie's snoring figure slumped in the chair. I sag to the floor next to her, leaning my back up against the wall. I'm sitting on a bunch of stuff, so I sweep it out from under me. A colorful piece of ripped paper catches my attention. It's a beat-up old cover of *A Tale of Gnomekind* that's been ripped off the book. Huh. There's a diagonal crease along one of the corners that looks just like the diagonal crease on the cover of my book. The one that was hanging on by a thread. The one I told Willy to stop touching because she was going to rip it.

I pick up the torn cover. Surely this can't be . . . I flip it over, and right there, in faded ink, is my name written on the other side, right where I put it all those years ago when Mom gave me the book. The weird thing (well, the additional weird thing to all the other weird things) is that there's other writing. I know I didn't write anything else, but there's definitely something. It looks like it's been partially erased or smeared away. The cover isn't exactly in mint condition.

Troll ~~cliff~~ has us

~~hereonup~~ a mountain

Pl~~easesend~~help

"Troll has a mountain. Pl—elp?" I say it softly, a whisper to myself. What the heck does *that* mean? And who wrote it? Could it have been Willy? I kept telling her to stop touching my book, and this is clearly my book, or rather, the cover from my book.

"What is that?" Smith looks down at my perplexed face.

"I'm not sure," I say. "I think it might be mine?" I look over to the Healer, who has been very quiet for the last few minutes.

"I found this thing," he says, pointing a long claw at the tattered cover. "In a biggie big bunch of leaves. I thought maybe it was a leaf, but no it was not. I picked it, thinking maybe a useful thing it could be. I don't know. Sometimes useful things fall through portals." He sweeps his arms out grandly, and I notice for the first time that a lot of the piles of junk everywhere are things from Topside. An empty soup can, one running shoe, a broken camping grill. I'm not sure how many of these things are useful, but I am also not a sweet-potato-faced yam man.

"Did you see anything else?" I ask. "Like maybe who

left this? Or did it come flying through the portal by itself?" I am still unclear about how the portals work. In the books, they don't exist. Everyone knows portals are kind of lame. I mean, it was cool in *The Lion, the Witch, and the Wardrobe*, but that was before EVERY book had them. Now it just seems kind of like lazy writing. Very critical, I know. My mom tells me that all the time. "Just enjoy the story, Buck, don't be so hypercritical." But I want everything to be smart and cool. Portals are not always smart and cool.

Smith snaps his fingers in front of my face. "Hello, spaceman. Still with us?"

"Sorry. Just thinking about portals."

"I know not where this thing came from," the little creature says. "I just liked the hat."

I flip the cover over to look at the illustration. I have seen it a million times, of course, but it's interesting to look at it through the eyes of someone (something?) who has never seen it before. Custard's hat is tall and pointy and red, but somehow it doesn't look dorky. Maybe because it's kind of dirty and the point just barely leans to one side. It somehow looks strong and cool, even though you know it's a red gnome hat.

"I like the hat, too," I say. I flip the cover back over.

"What do you think *Troll has a mountain. Pl—elp* means? I definitely didn't write that."

The Healer shrugs. Smith's eyebrows dive into a V shape as his forehead wrinkles in thought.

"It seems kind of crazy to think that my sister might have written it, but I think she did. I have no idea if she wrote it at home, though, or what." Suddenly my brain kicks into gear. "Hey!" I shout, standing up. Lizzie snorts in her sleep and turns her head away from me. The Healer bares his teeth like he might bite me. I hold up my hands in a peaceful gesture. "No! Just! Hear me out! What if Willy had this with her when she was taken and she's trying to send a message or something? What if this is a bread crumb or a clue?"

"That sounds a little far-fetched," Smith says. "The kids leaping through the portal were hypnotized. No hypnotized kid is going to be writing secret messages and leaving bread crumb trails. And if she wasn't hypnotized, she'd probably be catatonic from fright. No way she'd write some cryptic message."

I wish Lizzie wasn't out of it. I want to see what she thinks. Willy is kind of a wimp, true, but she's also supersmart and she's read more books that I have by about a million. And she carries that pencil around with her everywhere she goes, always tucked behind her ear. She might have been smart enough to leave a clue. Well, if she wasn't hypnotized.

For just a second my mind takes a step back and I think about what I just thought about. Willy. Kidnapped. Hypnotized. Trolls. I look around the room. Talking possum-yam. Actual gnome. Conversations about portals as real things no one questions. I feel light-headed again. How is this real? How is any of it happening?

"You're spacing out again, kid," Smith says. "What did you do to him?" He gives the Healer an accusing look.

"I did none of the things to him!" the Healer says in a huffy voice. "I fixed him!"

"Okay, okay," I say, doing my best to ignore their bickering. "Let's say this really is a message from Willy. And she really was trying to leave a clue about where she was being taken. What would be the next move here? How can we figure out where she is? As far as I know, there's no such thing as trolls owning mountains."

"May I remind you that I brought you here to find Macinaw?" Smith stares at me hard, pulls a small bug out of his beard, and cracks its exoskeleton between his teeth. I wince. "I've broken several important laws bringing you here, you know. And I showed you the Prophecy Room, which only a handful of gnomes have ever seen in the history of gnomekind. We are going to find Macinaw."

"Well, I'm not going to be here and *not* also look for my sister. Are you nuts?" He crunches the bug and I look away. "Don't answer that question."

"Look. Here's the deal, kid. Your sister is missing. I get that. You have all my sympathy." Smith looks like he has enough sympathy to fill a pen cap, with some room left over. "But the thing is, Macinaw is a big deal. His kidnapping has ramifications for our entire existence."

Now it's my turn to wrinkle up my forehead. "He's a cool guy and everything. His books are epic. But I'm not sure how his kidnapping is such an apocalyptic thing. Obviously, I would want to weep a million bitter tears if he didn't write any more books, but it's not like he's your king or leader or president or anything. I mean, his beard is awesome, but he's no Gandalf—and even the hobbits managed to mostly do fine without Gandalf for a while. Willy is my *sister*. She's my blood. MY world ends if I don't get her back. Don't you understand that?"

I pull my copy of *A Tale of Gnomekind* out of my back pocket and flip through it. Not like it's going to have all the answers or anything, it's just comforting to see those familiar words and phrases. It's comforting to see the gnome world that I know in my bones, rather than think about how this crazy place is in reality.

The creature looks at me with his shiny button eyes. "This one here is too big, eh? Too noisy, too." He looks me up and down. "You part troll? Eh?" He pokes me with a claw.

"What? No!" I say, taking a step back. "I'm not part anything, except part *awesome*." I puff out my chest to see if I can get Lizzie to laugh. She doesn't. She's still snoring—which means not dead, so I'm good with that for now.

"We should get out of here," Smith says abruptly. "Thank you, Healer, for everything you've done." He pulls a small bag from the bigger bag slung over his shoulder. It jangles and I can't help but smile. I'm in a place where they use real gold coins to pay for things? So cool.

The Healer shakes his head. "I not be needing that gold. I be needing that thing right there." He points a claw at Lizzie's busted phone, which is still somehow in my other hand.

Smith puts the gold back in his bag faster than you can say "cheapskate gnome."

"Sounds good to me," he says, smiling a real smile for maybe the first time since I met him. "Hand it over, Buck."

"Well, but . . . ," I say, looking over at Lizzie. "I can't just give it away without asking. That's not very nice. Plus, what if we get it working again? It's great as a flashlight, or a calculator, or . . ." The Healer has his hand out and is making a gimme motion. Smith has his arms crossed over his chest and is giving me A Look.

"Fine, fine." I give the broken phone to the Healer, who snatches it up with a squeal of glee. "Thank you for not killing Lizzie and for making sure I did not die."

There's a loud *whomp* behind me that nearly startles the smoothie right out of me. It's Katya. She's fallen through the hole and landed in a tangled clump. Her X suspenders are askew and missing at least half of their items. She's breathing hard, her eyes wide.

"We have a big problem," she groans.

Smith rushes to her, and that's when I notice she's hurt. Blood is seeping through the left side of her shirt, right under her gnome-ish rib cage.

"They're after us," Katya whispers, her eyes losing focus.

The creature drops down next to her and rips away the bottom part of Katya's shirt. I see a huge gash across her abdomen. It's the size of her whole belly, the bruise blossoming as we watch, blood dripping from the cuts of what I can only guess were knives? I swallow. Or claws?

Katya's eyes flutter. "They're right behind me."

11

"Who's after us?" I ask no one in particular.

The sweet-potato/possum creature is working fast, chewing on some kind of moss and spitting it into Katya's gashes. She's grimacing like it feels the way I think it feels.

"Who did this?" Smith asks.

"Shut up, all of you," Katya says, her eyes rolling. It looks like she's trying to stay conscious. "I hate you, Smith."

He grunts.

"But even so, I hate these trolls more." She grimaces and adds, "Plus, our fates are tied together now. They think I'm working with you. We are being officially pursued." She winces as the creature starts wrapping her belly with a tight, dirty-looking bandage.

"Officially pursued?" I ask. "Like with paperwork and wanted posters? That seems really organized for a bunch of trolls."

Katya is whispering something to Smith, and his face is grim. I keep talking because I don't know what else to do. "Is there anything we can do to throw these trolls off our trail?" I turn to the critter. "Can you make us invisible?"

Smith is still bent over Katya but looks up at me with a start. He bursts out laughing. "Did Macinaw write that in those books of his?"

Katya shakes her head. "Macinaw." She spits. Again. "What did he say in his books? The Healer paints invisibility on you? Throws a special blanket over your head?" Now she starts to laugh even as she winces and gasps.

I make Lizzie's badger face. "Macinaw never said anything about being invisible. I was just trying to help. There has to be some way we can throw the trolls off our trail, other than, you know, literally throwing them off our trail." I flex my arms where biceps should be. "I might need some gym time before we attempt that."

"I'm sorry I got you into this," Katya groans.

"It's okay," I say. "I mean, really, we got *you* into—"

"Not YOU, troll!" she yells at me. "The Healer." She holds her hand out to him and he squeezes it. "Those awful trolls will be after you, too, if they know you've associated with us."

"It's none of the big deals," the Healer says. "I will come along. I was needing to watch this girl-o, anyhoo. Make sure she keeps with the breathing and all that."

Smith pulls Katya to her feet. "We have to stop talking and start moving. Now." He turns to the creature. "How long until the poultice starts working for her?"

The creature looks at his wrist, which has no watch on it. "Maybe five of the minutes? Plus extra? Depends on the wound. Depends on the troll. Depends on the gnome—"

"Okay. I get it. You don't know." Smith puts a hand on the creature's shoulder. "How long until . . ." He motions to Lizzie, who's still snoozing in her chair.

"I can wake her now," the Healer says, snapping his claws in front of Lizzie's face. Her eyes flash open and she screams off and on like a car alarm. "I'm not so sure you want her awake just yet, though, yes?" he shouts over her screaming.

"Lizzie," I say, putting my hand on her arm. "Calm down. It's okay. You're safe." I pause. "Well, no. You're not really safe, but *we're* not going to hurt you. Right, guys?"

Smith, Katya, and the Healer all nod and smile with varying degrees of believability.

"You have to stop screaming," I say. "Okay? Right now. We have to go quickly. And quietly." I'm talking to her like I'm trying to coax a cat out of a tree.

Slowly her eyes start to focus on my face. She's taking deep gulping breaths. "What is THAT?" she gasps, and points at the creature. She pulls her legs up onto the chair.

"A friend," I say, pretty sure that's true. "We have to leave here now, though, all right? Can you come with me?" I'm still trying to talk calmly and slowly as I hold out my hand.

"Stop talking to me like I've had a lobotomy," Lizzie snaps. I smile broadly. There's my Lizzie.

She takes my hand and stands. Her palm is really sweaty.

"Before we leave," the Healer says, scratching through a pile of junk over in a corner, "This you should all use." He pulls out an envelope that looks like it's made of skin. I shiver. Then, before any of us can move, he starts dumping the contents of the envelope on our arms and shirts. It's a fine brown powder and it smells even worse than the poop smoothie.

"Ugh, what IS this?" I choke out.

"No, we don't need—" Smith starts, but it's too late. The Healer dumps a packet over his head.

"Rub it in good, now," the Healer says, rubbing it into his potato head. "All over your heads and faces and necky necks, too. There you go." We all start rubbing in the powder, and gagging as we do it.

I realize what we're doing. *"The trolls tracked Custard over mountainous terrain for days. Even as he crouched in impossible crevices, the trolls would peer in after him, dripping their slimy drool on his head as they waited for him to show himself and give up. Thanks to the powder, they could only catch the smallest scent of a gnome on the loose. He was protected, but only while the Stink lasted."* I quote from book two. "You *are* making us invisible," I say, lifting my chin and grinning. "Invisible to the trolls' noses. Ha!" I point at Smith. "I'm not so dumb after all. Burn!"

Smith's eyes are like white and black marbles standing out from the brown dust on his face. That makes it even more evident when he rolls them at me.

"Whatever, genius. Come on. We have to get out of here." Katya limps to the rope ladder leading up out of the hole and into the leaves. I follow, making sure Lizzie is ahead of me. Smith is behind me, and the Healer is behind him.

"Thank you," I say down the ladder to the yam-faced man thing. "My head feels much better now."

"As it should do," he says with a smile. "But watch your eliminations for a few days. That might get tricky on you."

My face falls. Wait. What?

"Come on, come on," Smith says before I have a chance to ask any more questions. He gives my butt a shove. "Let's get out of here. I don't want to be in the line of fire of those eliminations for any longer than I have to."

When Katya and Lizzie are through the hole, I poke my head up after them, forgetting momentarily about the pile of leaves that surrounds the hole. I pop my head up out of the leaves and see Katya hiding behind a tree off to my right. Her hand is over Lizzie's mouth and her face is as pale as the moon that's starting to rise.

Katya's eyes dart to the side and I see what she's looking at. A . . . herd? Band? Murder?—of trolls. They're standing off to the distance in a semicircle. They're huge creatures, with blue-hued skin. Some are dark blue, others lighter. They don't seem to have a lot of hair on their heads, but a couple have super-hairy chests like my dad. The biggest of them all has shiny golden hoop earrings. The books describe the trolls as ferocious and blinding blue, but these guys are dusty and dirty, and even though they're giant and scary-looking they don't really seem like monsters. It's hard to explain, but they just seem like . . .

blue football players. Except extra-giant.

Smith pushes out of the leaves beside me and takes in a sharp breath. "What are *they* doing here?" he whispers.

"Um, aren't they after us?" I whisper back.

"Long as we stay a-stinkin', no one'll ever find us," the Healer says in his loud squeaky voice as he emerges from the pile of leaves. I whip around and put my hand over his mouth, but it's too late.

The five trolls break their semicircle as they each turn their enormous bulk to see where the squeaking came from. But before they see us, there is a loud yell, and a cluster of gnomes, painted in camouflage, bursts from the bushes surrounding the trolls. The trolls seem surprised and weirdly unarmed.

"Never without their bludgeons and maces, the troll race is attuned to fight at all times, making them a difficult and cunning foe," I whisper to myself. This is a guiding rule of trolls.

Smith whips his head around and shushes me fiercely, his finger slicing up to his lips. The camouflaged gnomes are circling the trolls. "Don't move, you doorknobs," says a gnome who is lazily swinging a metallic-looking lasso over his head. "No need for any trouble." Wait. Is that a lasso made of *chains*? Yikes.

"Why not?" another gnome asks. He's holding one of those slingshot gun things. His deep black unibrow glistens with sweat. "Trouble is fun."

I expect that at any moment the trolls will just crush these gnomes; they'll flex their bulging muscles and wipe these guys off the planet. Instead, though—and this is super-weird—they're breathing really unevenly and heavily. The trolls are crowding closer and closer together, eyes looking up and down and all around like they can't quite settle on a way to escape. They look like my dog when we're trying to get him into the car to go to the vet . . . they seem scared.

How can these beasts, these gigantic, muscly monsters, be scared of anything, much less a handful of small gnomes?

"Get on your knees, you bag of hammers," Unibrow growls. The other gnome, swinging the lasso made of chains, whips it hard over their heads, making them flinch. Unibrow tosses a rock and hits one of the trolls in the back of the leg, causing him to stumble and fall to his knees. The gnome laughs and the troll gives him a murderous look but doesn't move from where he now kneels on the forest floor. That troll, on his knees, is about my height, maybe still a little taller. He turns his head and sniffs the air. I hold my breath and drop my head even lower behind the tree branch where I've been hiding. The troll trains his gaze right on my face, through the sparse leaves. For the first time I notice that his ankles are shackled. No wonder he fell so easily.

"Just stay quiet," the Healer chatters. "They never see us behind these trees. They never smell us with the stink powd—" I tap him on his small shoulder and point to the troll who's staring right at me. The troll's dark blue lips spread into a wide smile, his square yellow teeth glowing in the moonlight.

The Healer squints; then his eyes widen. "Oh," he whispers. He pulls a stub of a pencil from a fanny pack and makes a note on his wrinkly hand. "Add more of the stink to the stink powder," he whispers to himself.

Unibrow pushes himself behind the smiling troll and binds his hands with chains he's pulled from a bag on the ground. The troll howls. The other gnomes are doing the same thing. None of the trolls are putting up a fight. I don't understand. This big, ugly brute in front of me stops howling, sniffs, and smiles at me. It sends a shiver up my spine.

The gnomes kick at the trolls' bare feet, indicating they want them to stand back up, and soon the group is marching off into the dark forest, away from us, chains clanking.

The one troll turns his head around, still looking at me and still smiling. I can only imagine *he's* imagining how I would taste for dinner. Lucky that those gnomes were there to keep us from becoming troll food.

"We need to keep moving." Katya's voice is ragged, her breathing heavy. "It isn't safe here."

I want to say "Duh," but it feels like maybe this would be an inappropriate time. Mom would be very proud of me for thinking before talking. Man, I wonder what's going on back home. How long have we been gone, anyway? Could Mom and Dad still be in that weird sleep? Are alien Buck and Lizzie storming through the house, hunting for a Play-Station? I need to find Willy and get home. Being here, in this world, is amazing and everything, um, sort of. But it's not so fun when everything else is going wrong. I always read books and wonder why the main character isn't more excited to be marching through the labyrinth, or flying the spaceship in the big battle, but I guess it's because they're always searching for something or running from someone. No one ever gets to go on a cool quest for, like, vacation. There's never any time to really take in the scenery. What a bummer.

"Any ideas on where this Troll Mountain might be?" I hold up the now even more crumpled (*dang* it) book cover.

The daylight has faded, so it's hard to see the cover in the forest-darkened twilight. Lizzie looks at me blankly, dirt smeared on her face, in her hair. Her eyes are a little more focused now, but it's almost as if I can see the little birds flying around her head and making the *cuckoo* noises they do in cartoons. Smith is bruised and even grouchier than when he came to us Topside. Katya is obviously in pain, her teeth gnashed together, a sheen of sweat covering her face and sparkling in the moonlight. The only group member who doesn't seem exhausted or beat up is the Healer. He is smiling broadly and clapping his hands.

"It's possible Troll Mountain could be in Troll Nest," Smith says, frowning. "But from what I know of Troll Nest, it isn't mountainous. It's just a nasty place full of trolls. I guess Mackinaw could be there." I give him a look. "And your sister," he acquiesces. "But doesn't that seem a little . . . obvious?"

"Who cares if it's obvious?" I say. "At least it gives us a place to start."

"Or a place to die," Katya says with a grunt.

"To my home we go, we find a mappy map, and get some extra fixings for this lady gnome here, yeah?"

It's starting to dawn on me that at some point we're going to want to eat. And sleep. And go to the bathroom. I bet we can do all those things while we find some mappy maps at the Healer's house.

"Sure," I say. "Do you live close?" The thought of going to a house has suddenly made me starving. *All gnomes welcome fellows in their homes; it is the code of gnome-kind. Hospitality is a sign of a noble race.* I hope the Healer's people are also noble. I've had enough running for one day.

"We need to get somewhere fast," Katya interrupts. "Whatever that little scene was we just witnessed was something separate from—" But she doesn't have time to finish. A clod of dirt explodes on a tree trunk just above her head.

"Go! Go! Go!" Smith yells, and we all take off running after him. Man. So much running. I wonder if he knows where he's going. I throw a glance over my shoulder, but now it's too dark to see who's behind us.

"This way!" the Healer hollers, speeding up and over-taking Smith. He's a speedy little dude, I'll give him that. Katya is way behind us, unable to move fast because of her injuries. Lizzie runs back to her and lifts her up like she's Superwoman or something and throws her on her back, piggyback style.

The running footsteps behind us are light and fast. It has to be gnomes. There are so many creatures after us it feels a little hopeless, even as adrenaline makes me run faster than I've ever run before. The gnomes have weapons and will catch us soon—it feels inevitable. I can't run forever. And if they don't get us, the trolls are bigger and will surely be able to overtake us at some point. Have we already reached the part in the story when the hero seems to be at the point of no return? It seems early for that. Also—am I the hero? That makes me smile for a split second, before I realize this isn't a book and someone isn't writing a finely plotted story. This is real life. Who knows what's going to happen neeeeeeeeeeext.

I fall in a hole with an *OOF*.

12

The Healer leans over the edge of the hole, his eyes shining. "Good idea!" His whisper is loud. "Shortcut!" He leaps into the hole after me.

"Uh," I say, pulling myself up from where I've sprawled out on the muddy bottom of the hole. "Shortcut?"

Lizzie is breathing hard and leaning over the mouth of the hole now. Katya is still on Lizzie's back, her head lolling dangerously backward. How can her neck bend like that? It makes me grimace.

"Buck! Why are you in a hole? I thought we were going to the Healer's house."

"I'm not in here on purpose," I call back, feeling a little bad at sounding so testy. "I fell in."

Lizzie starts to laugh but then looks over her shoulder. "Oh, dang. Dang!" She leaps into the hole and, losing her footing, falls into the mud next to me. Katya sprawls out behind her, still unconscious.

There is a lot of shouting coming from up above, but I can't really make out what anyone is saying. It's definitely gnomes, though, and I recognize Smith's gruff blustering.

"Crazy!" I hear Smith shout; then there's a small bang, he says something else, then, "That way!" The footsteps go crunching off away from the hole. A few minutes later, Smith lands next to us.

"Next time you want to throw yourselves in a hole, can you warn me first? That was close."

I want to ask for more details, but the Healer is leaning over Katya and his little potato forehead is wrinkled in concern. "We gotta get this lass out of here fast fast. Great she is not doing." There is blood seeping through the bandages, and Katya's face is ghost white. Even though she nearly brained me, and she keeps calling me a troll, I still don't want her to die or anything. The thought makes me nauseous.

Lizzie gently picks Katya up again, and I am again amazed at how strong she is. I can barely carry my own self around—I can't imagine having another living creature on my back. "Which way?" Lizzie asks.

It appears we're just . . . in a hole. But the Healer says, "Follow me," and this crazy thing happens. His hands shoot forward, his claws vibrating in a way that makes them blur. Dirt and rocks start flying out behind him and we all take as many steps back as the hole will allow. I shield my eyes from the flying dirt and see he's already made significant progress tunneling out of the hole.

"How about that?" I murmur to myself. "I thought only gnomes were tunnelers."

"Is that what your books say?" Smith mutters. We are slowly following the Healer, far enough back that we don't get blinded by the flying dirt.

"My books say a lot," I counter. "But obviously they don't tell the whole story."

"Obviously, they don't tell the correct story," he says.

"They're fiction," I say, feeling a little huffy, like I have to defend Macinaw. "They aren't supposed to be true stories. At least, I don't think they are."

Smith makes a *hmph* noise, and the tunnel narrows as it goes deeper and the Healer speeds up. We move faster now, in single file. It feels like ages pass, eons, maybe. We are walking and walking and walking, and the tunnel is narrow, narrow, narrow, and I feel like at any moment I might freak out because my legs are going to fall off or the dirt is going to cave in and suffocate us all. I feel very unbrave. Is that a thing? Well, it is now. Buck Rogers: the Unbrave. These constant reminders that I am no hero are not very fun. I just want to find Willy and go home.

The Healer finally stops. He holds out a hand for us all to stop, too, and we do. It's only now, as Lizzie nearly nearly collapses into my shoulder, leaning so hard on me that I stagger a bit, that I realize she has been carrying Katya on her back this whole time. I was so busy being miserable, I never offered to help. I mean, she could have *asked* for help, though, right? Sigh. Way to go, Buck.

"I make us a way up right now. We should be in just the right place. Dark outside it is, but keep your heads low, yes? Yoomans and gnomey gnomes might make the people a bit skittish."

Everyone nods. Our eyes look super-white, standing out from our dirty faces. I'm so tired, this all feels like some kind of dream. I want to cry from the tiredness, and from . . . just . . . everything, which is super-embarrassing. I sniff hard as the Healer starts angling his digging upward. This, of course, means I snort a bunch of dirt into my nose, which then makes me cough and gag. Lizzie and Smith both look at me like they want to take my head off.

"Sorry," I whisper, and wipe the back of my hand over my nose.

It doesn't take long for the Healer to break the surface. He scrambles out of the hole and we follow. It's very dark up here, and the air is cool. I take huge gulps. I didn't realize how stuffy and musty it had been underground. On my second deep breath, I realize there's a tinge of smoke in the air. Not woodsmoke, something different. Something stinkier.

The Healer takes off at a galloping pace, without any warning at all. We all run after him, because what else can we do? We can't get lost in the dark. My breath is coming hard as I yet again feel a stitch in my side from running so fast. Didn't the Healer just say to keep our heads low? Jeez. Now we're all stumbling and grunting, exhausted and trying to keep up with him. I can't see much, but I can tell we aren't in a meadow and there is no forest around. There's dirt and dust under my feet, and some shadows in the distance that I think might be houses. Except most of them are smoking. There's a faint red glow coming from up ahead.

The Healer is fast. When we finally catch up to him, he's breathing heavily, and his head is spinning to and fro, like he can't figure out which way to go. There are more fires now, big bright flames, and the smoke in the air is thick. The Healer's eyes are huge, like Willy's when she sees a cockroach.

"My Erma," he says. "My Erma! What is happening?"

It seems super-weird that all of these places are on fire and there are no creatures or gnomes or trolls anywhere. It's a burning ghost town. That gives me shivers. The Healer takes off running again, and we follow. He stops suddenly, scraping at the dirt on the ground with his claws. There's a trapdoor. He lifts it up and jumps down into whatever is below. Without even thinking about it, I jump after him. Lizzie, Katya, and Smith are right behind me.

The trapdoor slams shut and there's a huge cloud of dust. There are shrieking noises everywhere. Arms and legs are flailing and people are yelling. I finally stop seeing stars from the sharp gnome elbow stabbing my stomach, and then I get a mouthful of a very dusty broom.

"Out, you devils!" a high-pitched woman's voice shouts. "Devils in my space! You get out now!" She whacks me again with the broom. The Healer is trying to stop her, but she's evading him like some kind of tiny, dusty ninja lady.

"Hey!" I protest, reaching out for the broom. "Stop it!" I grab the broom and give a yank. The woman holding it doesn't give it up without a struggle, but another couple of yanks gets it out of her hands and fully into mine. I toss the broom behind me and put my hands on my hips. As the dust settles I see that the yam-faced woman in front of me is the same size as the Healer. She has more hair than he does, though. It's pulled into two tufts on either side of her head, just above her ears. Her nose is pointier than his, giving her a combo weasel-yam look. Her hands are on her hips now and she's breathing fast. There's soot all over her clothes and face.

"What means this, Constantine?" she breathes. "WHAT MEANS IT?"

But the Healer doesn't answer. He's hugging the woman, lifting her from the ground and spinning her around. She is still shooting laser eyes at the rest of us, but finally she quiets down and buries her face in his shoulder.

After a moment, he releases her, and she is immediately down on her knees next to Katya, pulling her bandages off and grimacing. "Please to hand me romp root and tree frings. Now, Constantine!" the woman says in a commanding voice. The Healer crosses his arms over his chest, but then hurries across the dimly lit room and pulls two bunches of dried plants from the ceiling. He tosses them to the woman. She chews them up and spits them onto Katya's wounds. Katya groans and Lizzie gags.

"In trouble you will get us, Constantine," the woman

says. Her voice is calmer now, but still angry. She stands and flicks her hand. A flame shoots from one long talon-like claw. She lights several lanterns around the space, and I worry that having a fire in a room full of so many dried-up things is a bad idea. Surely, that's not how the rest of the village burned down, right?

"What is to keep this one here from telling the Syndicate about what you're doing? Bringing yoomans here!" She points her flaming finger at Smith. "You bring ruin onto this family, Constantine. That hut of yours? In the woods. A bad idea, I says. And I'm still saying it!"

The Healer is now beside Kayta, pulling new bandages tight around her. He asks if she's feeling better. She gives a weary nod but doesn't move from the dirt floor. He stands and wipes his hands on his pants.

"Erma, I keep the hut in the woods so's I don't blow up the shoppy shop when I test out the new things. Without that hut these guys I would not have found." He motions at us, as if there are other guys hanging around. "These here are critters that need our help. They not bring hurt to us. They help us." He pauses for a second and then quietly, through gritted teeth, he says, "I like my hut."

Erma does not seem to agree with the Healer's assessment.

"These yoomans mixed up with troll blood?" she asks,

poking me in my stomach and then backing away. She steps closer to Lizzie and looks her up and down. "Seem too pretty-like to be mixed up with the troll blood." Lizzie blushes and takes a step back.

The Healer's eyes move from me to Lizzie, sparkling in the lantern light. "They are yoomans come to fulfill that prophecy." Everything in the room is still for a moment. No one makes a sound. I feel a trickle of sweat slide down the side of my face.

"You are the one, then," Erma says. Her voice is quiet, shaking. "You are why they came. Why they burned everything. They said they was looking for someone, that we were hiding someone. We say no, but . . ." She shakes her head. "When they not find what they was looking for, they chase everyone away. I ran here. Hid away from them and those terrible torchy torches they had."

"Soon as I see the smoke, I knew you'd be smart like that," the Healer says. He tries to smile, but his eyes are very sad. "Lucky we have this place."

Erma nods and leans her head on his shoulder. "This is all we have now."

I feel like I shouldn't look at them while they're huddled together like this. I feel like it's my fault this village is burned to a crisp. I can only look at the dirt floor, feeling miserable.

My cheeks burn with embarrassment at intruding on their private moment, and I burn hot and itchy inside because I know this wouldn't be happening without me.

Lizzie pinches me on the arm. Not hard, but just enough to get my attention. She motions with her head to a farther, darker corner of the room and I follow her. The room isn't very big, and the rounded dirt ceiling is low. There's a curtain that makes up the far wall. I guess this is like some kind of storage place. I saw a movie once where a house had a basement and inside the basement there were all these shelves of homemade jelly and pickles and stuff. This reminds me of that, except smaller, and with a lot of dried plants hanging from the ceiling and tickling my head.

"Who do you think burned down the village?" Lizzie asks in a whisper. "Do you think they were really looking for us?" Her face is dirty, her mouth bent in a frown.

"They were looking for me," I say. "Katya said the trolls were right behind her—they must have figured out I was with the Healer and come here looking for me. Lucky I'm so slow."

Lizzie's eyes narrow just a bit, like they do just before she yells at me. She doesn't say anything else, though, just sighs and looks over at the Healer and his wife, who are holding on to each other tightly.

Smith clears his throat and approaches them. "I promise we shall bring no harm to you," he says. His voice is very stilted and formal. "You are offering refuge for injured gnomes and cannot be prosecuted."

Erma seems to relax at this, but only for a moment. Her eyes narrow, but she doesn't come closer to Smith. "How do we know this? How do we know you won't turn on us?"

"He offers his Gnome Pledge!" I blurt. *"By the rites of the ancients and the rites of the new guard, the gnomes pledge to do honor and protect all who need protection."*

Smith sighs and tries for a grimacing smile. "Yes. I offer my Gnome Pledge. Now, please, no more broom attacks."

"They are not gnomes," Erma says, pointing a claw at me and Lizzie. "Your pledge offers no protection."

Smith shifts from one foot to the other and looks to the Healer for help. We all know Erma is right.

"I think we all go have a bite to eat," the Healer says. "We rest up for a tiny bit of a bit. Then we plan what comes next." Erma gives him a grouchy look but motions for us to follow her. Lizzie and I help Katya to her feet.

We push through the curtain in the back of the room and into a darker, even more cavelike room. It's much cooler. Little flames burn in cracks along the ceiling. There are a tiny couch and tiny chairs, a table in the corner, and rugs on the hard-packed dirt floor. It's a comfortable-looking place.

Lizzie and I lay Katya on the couch, and Smith takes a seat in an overstuffed chair. The Healer goes to the back of the room and bustles around, clinking glass and slamming drawers. He returns with a tray of little sandwiches that look like what my mom calls finger sandwiches. Those usually have cucumbers in them. These look like they might actually have fingers. The Healer also has a bunch of tiny glasses of bubbly brown stuff. Lizzie and I sit on the rug and each take a couple of sandwiches and a glass. Erma does not sit. She stands and peers down at us, her arms crossed over her tiny barrel chest.

The Healer fills her in on the story while we eat. I don't even care if these sandwiches do have fingers in them, they are super-tasty and I want to eat a million of them. At one point Erma leans down to inspect my head and then gazes hard into Lizzie's pupils. She nods but doesn't say anything. When the Healer is finished he gives her a sheepish sort of smile.

"So now I adventure on with these guys. Hunted we are. But this guy," and here he points at me, "win the freedoms for all the critters Flipside."

"And what about the oppressors?" Erma says, staring at Smith. "They aren't gonna like that."

"Yes, well." The Healer looks nervous all of a sudden. He goes up to Erma and puts his arm around her waist. He leads her from the room, leaving us alone.

Smith licks crumbs off his fingers and then takes a sip of his bubbly drink, makes a face, and sets the glass on a little table next to his chair. I sniff at my drink. Compared to everything else the Healer has given me to ingest, sandwiches notwithstanding, it smells pretty good. Like ginger ale and licorice. I take a sip. Not bad, really, but there is an alarming hot dog aftertaste. I set the glass down.

The Healer and Erma come back into the room, each carrying a stack of maps.

"You need a plan, yooman," the Healer says, plopping his stack of maps on the floor in front of me.

Erma sets her stack of maps down in front of Lizzie.

"Maps," she says, and for the first time offers a small smile. She sees me peering down at my glass and says, "You like the peaberry tea?"

"It's a little weird, but mostly okay," I say, smiling back at her. "Thank you."

"Good, good. Troll sweat and the peaberries will make you strong."

Smith starts laughing and I feel my stomach twist.

"T-troll sweat?"

Erma smiles and shakes her head. "How else do you think I make the peaberry tea, silly yooman?"

I push my glass farther away and feel my face go a little pale. There's nothing in the books about troll sweat or anything called peaberries. And really . . . it just now occurs to me that there is no mention of this village in any of the Triumphant Gnome Syndicate books. I wrack my brain, trying to think of even the slightest mention of a town made up of tiny creatures, but I come up with nothing.

"A compendium of truths, I offer you here, my dear reader. Tales of truth and bravery and adventures never before seen by human eyes. I present to you the stories of Flipside and all of our peoples."

Everyone is staring at me. Oops. I didn't mean to say that out loud.

"It's from the introduction to book one," I mutter. "*A Tale of Gnomekind*? I was just wondering why Macinaw never mentioned this village in any of the books. Especially since he said he was telling us about everyone in Flipside."

"The books are fiction, Buck," Lizzie says. "He can tell whatever stories he wants." She blinks at me. Am I being exasperating?

Smith is in a chair, his head leaning back, his eyes closed. "The girl is smarter than she looks," he mutters.

Lizzie gives him a sour look, even though he can't see her.

I look at the stack of maps in front of me. I'm not sure I have the energy to go digging through these things. I'm not even sure what I'm looking for, other than something that could be called Troll Mountain. Maybe we should get some sleep and then look at the maps.

A soft snore comes from Smith. Katya is already asleep—or unconscious. Without another word, Erma disappears and comes back with an armload of empty fabric bags. "This place is not really meant for the sleepings," she says. "But have these things, I do. For delivery of my poultices." It's really very kind of her to be sheltering us like this, putting herself, and everything she and the Healer own (or what's left of it), in danger.

I take a couple of the bags and tell her thank you. I roll one up like a pillow and lay the other one over my legs. They smell really weird, like hay and some kind of rotten fruit. But I'm not going to complain. Not even as I fall asleep on this dirt floor with tiny bugs that seem super-stoked to eat whatever is left of the stinky fruit juice, or just whatever is available of me.

13

I wake up to shouting. Lots and lots of shouting. The curtains are shut, separating the back room from the room with all the poultice supplies, but it doesn't do much to block out the noise. The light in here is still very dim, and I have no idea how much time has passed. The inside of my mouth feels like I spent a significant amount of time sucking on sandpaper in my sleep.

Lizzie's eyes are shining in the near-dark from her pallet on the other side of the chair where Smith still snores. Katya's eyes are closed, too, and her bandages look pretty gross, but it doesn't look like fresh or new grossness, so that seems like good news. Lizzie's eyes meet mine. What in Hob's pants is going on out there? We don't have time to guess. The curtain swings aside and four gnomes appear, dressed in clothes very similar to the camo stuff the gnomes in the forest were wearing.

"Sheriff Smith, we are here to relieve you of your duty, sir!" one of the gnomes shouts, while the other three move swiftly to Smith. He startles awake and is immediately on his feet in an impressive sound-asleep-to-wide-awake-in-one-second movement. His tiny whip is in a pocket on the side of his pants, and his hand dangles there, like a cowboy in the Wild West ready to grab his gun for a shootout.

"You and your companions need to come with us." The gnome doing the talking, who I guess is the boss of the others, looks at me like you might look at a big pile of dog poo. What is the deal with these mean gnomes? Are they *so mad* that Lizzie and I were in the Academy that they hunted us down all the way out here? They're *so mad* that they want to relieve Smith of his duty? The gnomes in the books would never be like that. They'd be grumpy, sure. But then everyone would have a Colossal Sit-Down and work things out. This is super-weird. And scary.

Lizzie eases her way closer to me as everyone else in the room remains motionless. I can hear little squeaks from the Healer standing behind me near the now open curtain.

Lizzie leans over and whispers in my ear, "I don't like

this. We need to get out of here. I wish we knew how to call Johnny O'Sprocket. Maybe he could use his rainbows to distract these guys." I snort quietly. Like that would work. Lizzie frowns at me. I don't care what she says, I will never think Johnny O'Sprocket is cool.

Lizzie's frown turns thoughtful. She says, "Book one, when Custard is captured by the Troll Queen's minions."

I stifle a smile and give her a very small nod. Now, *this* is a good idea. Of course, my heart is banging around in my chest like someone dropped it down a flight of stairs, and I have no idea if this will work. Not to mention the fact that Smith, Katya, the Healer, Erma . . . none of them will have any idea what I'm doing. I can only hope—gah! Stop thinking about it too much, Buck. Lizzie is right. We need to get out of here. Just do it. Just do it!

I rush at the gnome who appears to be the leader, and I grab his hand with both of mine. I start shaking it like he's the president of the United States. "I am so glad you're here!" I shout, which, of course, is exactly the opposite of the truth. "It is such an honor to meet you." I'm pumping his arm up and down while Lizzie slowly gathers up the stacks of maps and signals for everyone to stand up. Hopefully, all eyes are on me and not her. "I never thought we'd get this chance!" I yell, puffing out my chest, trying to look big and strong and excited. "You look so different in person! And you brought friends!" The other three gnomes are staring at me, their weapons aimed but their expressions puzzled. Is it working? Custard was able to just loudly compliment all the trolls until he backed his way out of the room and ran for his life. I am not sure gnomes are as dumb as trolls, though.

As I shake the gnome's hand, I'm trying to turn him so that he stops blocking our way to the outer room. "I have heard stories about you!" I fake a loud belly laugh and shove one of his shoulders, while still shaking his hand with one hand. "You are such a crazy guy!" The other three gnomes are kind of smiling now. One of them nods and rolls his eyes at the leader. "I've heard you can really demolish your opponent in Tunnel Match. Straight down the pitch, drop into a hole, fast as lightning." The gnome isn't sure what to do with me, I can tell. He is one hundred percent confused. Lizzie is holding a stack of maps in her arms, with Smith right behind her. They are inching closer to me. Katya is up now, right behind them, and the Healer and Erma are conferring in a corner.

"What do you think of the LowLand Devils?" I ask. "I think they stink."

"Whoa ho," one of the other gnomes says, breaking

into a smile that every sports fan wears when trash talk starts. "Be careful what you say there, friend. Those could be fighting words." His weapon goes slack as his arm drops to his side and he opens his mouth to say more. The gnome next to him elbows him in the arm, and he clears his throat and lifts his weapon back up, pointing it at me.

"Anyway," I say loudly. "It's been super-great to finally get to meet you. We need to be going now." I strong-arm him into taking a couple of steps to the side so that Lizzie and Smith and Katya can squeeze past us into the outer room. Out of the corner of my eye I see the Healer giving Erma a tearful hug, and then he scampers by. "Okay. Well, it was my pleasure to spend these precious few moments with you, sir. I hope you have a very nice day." I let go of his hand and run into the outer room, whispering, "Go, go, go!" Smith and Katya are already halfway up the ladder when the leader gnome yells, "Hey! Wait a minute!"

This time I don't whisper. "Go! Go! Go!" The Healer leaps onto the ladder and flies after Smith and Katya. Lizzie is standing at the bottom of the ladder trying to figure out how to climb it and hold a giant stack of maps. The gnomes burst into the room, weapons pointed.

"Just go!" I yell, and Lizzie drops the maps, clambering up the ladder as fast as she can. I stare at the stack scattered across the floor, trying to decide which one I can stuff down down my pants; which one is the most important, most valuable; which one will get us to Willy and the Troll Vanquishing Mace—when a clod of dirt explodes right next to my ear.

"*Aaah!*" I yell, and I forget about the maps. I fling myself up the ladder, kicking out as small gnome hands with sharp fingernails grab at my ankles.

"Out, you devils!" Erma yells, and I hear the sounds of her broom smacking the gnomes. I throw myself out of the trapdoor just as the first gnome appears behind me. Under him, I see the other gnomes grabbing up the maps and racing to the ladder.

"Buck!" Smith shouts, and I follow his voice, running hard, thankful for a good night's sleep to give me energy to keep moving. I mean, my legs still feel like they're made of tree trunks, and my head aches, but I'm not as exhausted as I was yesterday, so that's a start.

I find Smith and everyone else behind a smoldering hut. The gnomes are right behind us, so we run, darting across the village in zigzags, like butterflies do to confuse predators. Finally, we manage to drop behind a scorched boulder that's behind a blackened cottage. The gnomes run by, checking behind the cottage. One of them has the maps stuffed in a bag on his back. Thankfully, they seem consumed by the idea that we're in a cottage, and they don't look behind the big rock. They fly off past us, swearing and shouting.

The air is hot and dusty and a wild wind whips my hair, bringing along with it a scorched smell, like the inside of a dirty oven. It feels like an oven out here, too. My eyes are watering as they adjust to the bright sunlight. It looks like we've popped up on the edge of a market—or what a market would be based on what I've read, and what I can imagine, since I have never actually been to a fictional outdoor market *and* pretty much everything out here is a smoldering wreck. There are blob-shaped stalls leaning up against each other, and there are little burned-out booths in the middle of everything. Half-burned things hang in what's left of the booths, or are in heaps on the ground. Dust and ash are everywhere.

We pant in the shadows, trying to be as quiet as we can. I can't believe we left the maps. I can't believe the gnomes have them. Argh! "Such a wasted trip," I mutter to myself. "We put Erma in even more danger, and for what? No reason."

Lizzie gives me a steely look. "Well, Katya got some medicine," she whispers. "And we all got some food and rest. That has to count for something, doesn't it?"

"That's not what I meant," I whisper back. I wonder if Lizzie keeps hearing things I'm not actually saying. Or maybe I'm saying things that sound different in my head?

We wait for a few more minutes. No sign of the gnomes. There's no sign of any living thing, actually. Though the gnomes can't be too far ahead of us. I pull out my copy of *A Tale of Gnomekind*. The map in the book is the only map we have now. A few days ago I would have sworn that of course it's one hundred percent accurate, but now I have no idea. We're standing in a place that isn't even on it. The meadow is on the map, and the Academy. There's a forest labeled Forest of Unspeakable Things, which is weird because I'm pretty sure the only forest in Flipside is the Darkest Forest. There's also a bunch of unlabeled space off in the margins. To the north of the forest is the seashore, and to the east of it is Troll Nest, the City of Trolls. Well beyond that is a big bunch of nothing. Maybe that's where we can find Willy. And Macinaw. The trick, though, is figuring out where we are right now on this map. Hmm. It looks like no matter what, we're going to have to make our way through the forest. So that should be fun. I stuff the book back in my pocket.

Lizzie takes my hand on one side while the Healer takes

my hand on the other. Smith and Katya are behind us. We move slowly, sticking to the side of the market, moving among the shadows. A tiny creature that looks a lot like the Healer brushes past me pushing a cart filled with something like giant turnips. He eyes Smith and Katya warily and then hitches the hood of his cloak over his head, concealing his face.

Once the burned huts start to thin and there isn't much around other than dust and dirt and small trees here and there, I find a shady spot under one of the trees and pull out the book again.

"Where do you think we are on this map?" I ask Smith.

"It's not a real map," he says with a shrug. "We could be anywhere."

"It's the only map we have," I answer, feeling grouchy. "It can't be *all* wrong. Macinaw got *some* things right in his books."

"Give me that, troll." Katya snatches the book out of my hands and holds it close to her face. She turns it upside down and stabs her finger at the page. "Here. This is where we are."

"How do you know?" Lizzie asks. She peers down at the map. Her face is open, her mouth parted in a slight smile. I think, for some unknown reason, she really likes Katya.

Katya shrugs much like Smith did. "I just know. It feels right."

"And so finding my sister now comes down to a gnome's gut feeling. Excellent." I take the book back and put it in my pocket, sighing. "I think we should get those maps back from the gnomes who stole them. We can use this map"—I pat my pocket—"to get to Troll Nest. Then those other maps will have all the details we need. We'll steal them back, get to Troll Nest, find Willy and Macinaw, and then boom. Done."

"We better find the mace first if we're just gonna traipse into Troll Nest," Smith says with a shake of his head.

GAH. The Troll Vanquishing Mace. I forgot about that.

"Well," I say, trying to cover up that I forgot. "Obviously we're going to find the mace first. Probably its location is on one of those maps."

"Of course it is, Buck. Because life is always as easy as that! Let's get started!" Smith gives me an exaggerated thumbs-up, with a big fake grin on his face. His sarcasm drips out of his mouth like slimy drool.

"You know, when Captain Kirk gets lost on a planet, he always seems to be in control of things. And people listen to him. Only Spock gives him any argument, and it's always very polite. You guys need to watch more *Star*

Trek." I shove my hands in my pockets and try not to pout. I *want* to be a hero and no one is letting me be one.

"Are we going to try to get those maps back, or what?" Lizzie asks. "If we are, we're doing a very bad job of chasing the gnomes who have them."

"The maps are the key to everything," I say, not really knowing that for sure. But my mom always says that if you act confident you'll feel confident, so I'm testing out that theory. "I bet they say where the mace is, too. Let's go get them."

We all seem to be in agreement, though no one is jumping around in stoked excitement. Everyone seems kind of lost and irritated. I mean, we did just avoid being killed or captured by angry gnomes, but still.

"Come on, you guys!" I say, trying to remember *every* cheerleader movie I've seen—which is precisely one. "We're a team now, and we can do this." I throw my hand out. "Everyone put your hand on top of mine and when I say three we'll all yell, 'Go, team!'"

Lizzie puts her hand on mine, Katya puts her hand on Lizzie's, the Healer climbs on Lizzie to get his hand on the pile, and then finally Smith adds his, though he's rolling his eyes.

"One! Two! Three! GO, TEAM!"

I try to push everyone's hand up into the air in a kind of hand explosion/firework movement, but nobody has any idea what I'm doing, so it's all a little weird. That's okay, though, because we're all in this together. We are going to go find some maps! Woo!

As the trees close in on us, making it almost as dark as nighttime, Katya says, "Stay close and keep your wits about you. Unless you enjoy dragons roosting in your hair and cyclopean fleas gnawing on your face." She says she's tracking a path through the woods made of broken twigs and torn leaves. It's nothing I can see, but she seems sure it's from the gnomes with the maps.

"Nasty biters, the big fleas," says the Healer with a shiver. He's scraping a bit of gunk off a rock and putting the gunk into his fanny pack.

"I guess you can't snap your whip and open up one of those Snow White witch portals so we can see where the gnomes with the maps went?" I give Smith a hopeful look.

The gnome shakes his head. "My weapon is from an ancient magic, Buck." He rolls his eyes. "It can't just conveniently move the story ahead. In *real* life, I mean."

"Of course not," I mutter. "We wouldn't want anything to be convenient." Then I add aloud, "Good thing Katya is on our side," with a smile that I hope doesn't look as forced as it feels. "She seems great at sniffing out trails." I look helplessly at the foliage all around us. The foliage that looks exactly the same, no trail in sight. "Keep up the good work!"

"I don't need your permission to be a leader, troll," she says, pushing past me. Lizzie pushes past me, too, and shakes her head like she's disgusted with me as well. What did I say? Jeez.

"Hey!" I chase after them, catching up and then stopping to take off my glasses. I wipe all the grime and gunk on my shirt. "You know I'm not trying to be a jerk, right? I'm just trying to be the leader. Like, if this was a story, I would be all brave and issuing orders and—"

Lizzie looks at me with narrowed eyes. "It's not a story, Buck. How many times do we have to say that? It's real life. If it was a story, you'd already have been eaten. I mean, look at your shirt." I look down at my shirt. It's the same one I wore to bed however long ago that was. My

Triumphant Gnome Syndicate shirt. My *red* Triumphant Gnome Syndicate shirt.

"Oh, no!" I gasp. "*I'M* the red shirt!"

Lizzie tries to make her face look really serious, but her eyes are laughing. She nods slowly.

"DANG."

Now she laughs out loud and throws her arm over my shoulder. "I think you're going to be fine. Like I said, it's way past time for a red shirt to be eaten or swallowed by some quicksand."

I nod, but I still feel a little uneasy. "You know, if this is really called the Forest of Unspeakable Things, maybe we should keep our eyes open for some—"

A half grin appears on Lizzie's face. "R.O.U.S.s?"

I grin back and do my best Westley voice. "Rodents of Unusual Size? I don't think they exist." The Healer scampers up to us with a smile that shows off his sharp rodent-like teeth. Lizzie and I look at him and look at each other and burst out laughing. He gives us a curious look and then points to the sky. We look up and our laughing stops immediately. Flying in front of the sun is a cluster of . . . what? Birds? Bats?

"Dragons," the Healer whispers.

Can those *really* be dragons? I know I should probably

stop being amazed that these crazy things are all real, but *dragons? For real?*

"That is bananas," Lizzie says, her hands in her hair. "Totally bananas."

"But baby dragon season is in the high heat of the summer," I whisper, remembering book two.

The Healer shakes his head and whispers back, "Baby dragon season is all of the seasons."

"Why are we whispering?" whispers Lizzie. "Can they hear us?"

I feel a shiver crawl down my spine, but I shake it off. "We better keep moving," I say in my regular voice. "If we don't want to be dragon breakfast." Maori's brother was dragon breakfast in book two. I'd rather not see if that's one of the true parts of the books.

We jog to catch up to Katya and Smith, and as we do the Healer flicks a claw and a flame shoots from its tip, lighting our way. We follow a trail of bent branches. Katya and Smith silently trudge forward, moving slowly because of Katya's injuries and because the forest is so thick with trees and vines and these bush things that are full of thorns that seem to reach out to scratch you just for fun.

I have no idea how to judge distance, but when we've been moving long enough for me to be sure there's a blister the size of South Dakota on my heel, Smith stops suddenly. He looks around slowly and then nods once.

"We take a five-minute break. If anyone needs to . . . you know . . . don't go far and make sure to cover up your leavings."

It takes me a minute to figure out what he means. "Gross," I mutter, but then I step away from the group, because he's right. There will be no truck stop bathroom breaks on this journey.

Katya points to a tree branch that's missing leaves. "See?" she says to Lizzie. They're a little bit ahead of me and Smith. The Healer is far behind. I'm afraid he might be digging in the holes with our leavings so he can make disgusting potions. Grossss.

"The leaves are broken in a nonuniform way. Fresh, too," Katya continues. She picks off a broken leaf and shows Lizzie. I scramble up behind them and see that the crack in the leaf is a bright green line. "See how they're all broken here?" Katya says, pointing to the tree from which she just took the leaf. "And there," she says, pointing to a tree ahead of us, with more broken leaves.

"Wow, it really *is* a trail," Lizzie says. I can hear the awe in her voice and it makes me feel itchy inside. I mean,

Katya is pretty impressive with her tracking skills, but still. Awe? Really? It all just looks like . . . trees . . . to me.

"How do you know it's the gnomes leaving this trail?" I ask, weaseling my way between them as they walk.

Katya turns to me and smiles, her little square teeth gleaming in a beam of sunlight filtering through the trees. "I don't," she says. Then she shrugs, still giving me the same smile Willy does when she's up to no good. "Could be a bear. Dragon. Anything."

"Um" is all I can think to say.

Katya laughs. Hard. She seems to be feeling a lot better.

Lizzie links her arm in mine and I feel a lot better, too. I pull the ratty paperback from my pocket and flip to the map. "If we're really in the Darkest Forest—" Katya shoots me a look. "I'm sorry, I mean the Forest of Unspeakable Things. If we're really here"—I point to the map—"then there's a little town not too far away called Gloryville. Maybe the gnomes are there?"

Smith has caught up to us and he throws out a laugh like a bark. "Gloryville? You mean Glowerton. It's one of the sky towns, full of the meanest gnomes this side of the seashore. They mine fire sap from the trees, use trolls to do the heavy work."

"Nasty business, fire saps," the Healer says. He's run

up alongside us, his fanny pack bursting with who knows what.

"If the gnomes we seek are in Glowerton, we're going to need to be very careful," Smith says.

"*Of course* we're going to need to be careful," I say. Then I laugh. "You're talking just like Custard, with your blockbuster movie clichés. *Do you want a whip-down? Yeah, I thought you did.*"

Smith snarls. "I have never said anything that dumb."

"You just did!" I say, laughing.

"Okay, okay," Lizzie says, blinking at me. "Let's just get to Glowerton and get the maps before we kill each other. Cool?"

We walk in silence for a long time. I'd know how long if we still had Lizzie's phone, or, you know, if I HAD MY OWN PHONE. Eventually, we stop at a little stream for a drink and a rest.

"Should we really drink this?" I ask, looking down at the rushing, sparkling water. "Remember when that guy at school got some kind of amoeba or tapeworm or something when he drank from a stream in Venezuela?"

Lizzie sighs deeply. "We are not in Venezuela, Buck."

"I know! I'm just saying. Who knows what microscopic things live in—"

Lizzie slurps a huge handful of water while staring me down. Now it's my turn to sigh deeply. "Well, I can't let you drink it and me not drink it. Thanks a lot," I say.

"Let," Lizzie says, and shakes her head, standing up and walking out of the stream.

"What?" I say, following her, but any argument I might have is wiped from my mind. Up ahead I see the faint glow of lights way up in the trees. And I hear distinct flapping noises in the sky a little closer to us. Glowerton. Dragons.

"This will be very simple," Katya says, looking up. "Ride a dragon into Glowerton, find the maps, ride the dragon to safety."

"Simple?" I choke out. "How exactly does one *ride a dragon*?" I can't stop thinking about how Maori's brother was dragon elevenses in book two.

"You put your rear end on the dragon, you ride the dragon," Smith says, looking at me like I'm as smart as a human rock.

"We must be stealthy about this," Katya says, stating the obvious as gnomes apparently like to do. "If too many of us go up there, it will be chaos. We will have casualties."

"Okay," Lizzie says, clapping her hands together. "Buck and I will do it. Time to fetch some maps."

I put my hand on her clapping hands and lower them.

"I'm going to do this on my own." My voice is as serious as it's ever been. Katya is feeling better, but still technically hurt, so she can't go. The Healer is too loud. We need Smith on the ground as protection in case something goes wrong, and something will definitely go wrong. I will go alone. I can't have Lizzie getting hurt again. No way.

"What?" The excited energy drains from her face. She blinks at me, but her blinks don't work this time. I'm not being crazy. I'm dead serious.

"I'm going by myself. I can't risk anything happening to you, Lizzie. You've already been hurt once." I shake my head. "No way am I letting you do this with me. I need you safe and healthy. Right?" I look to Smith and Katya. The Healer is off to the side tasting mushrooms.

"Buck Rogers!" Lizzie shouts at me, taking me completely by surprise. "Who in the world do you think I am?"

I stare at her, eyes wide in shock. She is so mad it's making her hair shake.

"ANSWER ME!" she shouts. "Who do you think I am?!"

"Uh," I say, taking a step back. I mean, whoa. Why is she so angry? I'm trying to protect her. Does she *want* to get set on fire by dragons? Burned by whatever the heck fire sap is? Yikes. "Uh," I say again, losing all my grave-faced seriousness from before and replacing it with bald-faced confusion. "You're . . . you're my Lizzie. You're my best friend."

"No!" She points her finger at me. "You think I'm your sidekick. You think I'm your adorable and hilarious comic relief." She takes a deep breath, and that calms down her shaking voice. "I'm here to find Willy, too. I love Willy, too. I'm here for adventure, too. I'm amazed and shocked at how this is a real world and it doesn't match the books. I'm all of these things, too, Buck! I'm not just your cute Lizzie hanging around to give you a reason to feel like a brave hero."

"Lizzie—" I start, but she interrupts me.

"You know what I think? I think you're buying into all of this prophecy talk. You keep calling it stupid, but every time someone says something about it I see your face. I see the light come on in your eyes. I see how much you love it. Well, fine. FINE. Just admit it, though, okay? Admit you think it's awesome that this whole stupid freaking prophecy is about you. Yes, another story about a boy who's the answer to a prophecy. Congratufreakinlations."

Now it's my turn to blink a lot, because what the heck? I'm just trying to keep her from getting eaten by dragons. And I DO think the prophecy is stupid.

"We're not in a story." It's the only thing I can think to

163

say. "*You keep telling me that. It's not a story.*"

"We need to get going," Katya says. "The daylight will be gone soon, and we need to try to be out of the forest before nightfall."

The Healer gives a shiver. "All the creepy creepies come out at nighttime. In one bite they eat us all. Yum yum."

"I'm going by myself," I say.

"You are not the boss of this operation," Lizzie retorts.

"No one is the boss!" She's making me feel as exasperated as I do when Willy won't listen to me about how many times you hit the A-B combo to flick the Troll Vanquishing Mace at the Troll Queen in the online game. It's six times. SIX TIMES.

"Buck will go," Smith says. "Everyone else stays down here." He looks at me. "Get in and get out. Don't mess up."

I swallow hard. Okay, so maybe this hero stuff is a little more complicated than it seems in books and movies. But also . . . maybe I'm more prepared than other heroes? "*The dragon flew to Custard and nipped at his beard. Custard reached out to pet it on the head and the creature reared back, nearly incinerating Custard's hand—and beard—with one angry breath. 'Never touch a dragon, son,' said old Master Hob. 'You've yet to take dragon studies at the Academy, I see.'*"

"It's very odd when you do that," Katya says. "Quote from those books, I mean."

"Those books have taught me all I know of Flipside," I say. "They're my guide while I'm here."

Lizzie rolls her eyes so hard I'm afraid they won't roll back.

A small flock of dragons is way, way up high, above our heads. They are glowing faintly about the eyes and making quiet shrieking noises.

"I can get you hovering just above the flock and then will drop you. It will be your responsibility to grab on to a dragon as you fall toward them," Katya says.

"Uh," I say. "Wait. What?"

15

"Their vision is bad, but their smell is keen. Try to fall away from their snouts," Katya says. She raises a hand and the next thing I know, I'm flying up in the air on an invisible elevator ride. I try to stifle my *"AHHHHHH!"* so I don't scare the dragons away. In a quick moment I fly up past the dragons. In the same moment I get a closer look at the dragons, and the bottom falls out of my belly. This can't be right. Katya and Smith should have known. Why didn't they think?! I want to yell to Katya to stop, to let me down, but I'm too high up. The treetops are thin around me. I can actually see the sun in one warm, glorious minute. Then the wind is gone and I'm plummeting right toward the flock of dragons. Tiny dragons. Dragons the size of flying dachshunds. HOW am I supposed to grab on to one of these things? If I try to sit on it like a horse I'm going to break its back, or it's going to sink like a stone in a lake. These are the thoughts flying through my head as I hurtle toward the little dragons.

"*Aaaahhhhhh!*" I yell as I throw my arms out. I catch two dragons, one under each arm. It's like I'm dangling between two flying loaves of bread. Each has a wing squashed up against my side, while the other wings flap furiously next to my arms. The dragons are not happy with the situation, which is fine, because I am not happy with it, either. How could Smith and Katya not tell me they're so tiny?

The little dragons are sputtering and snorting smoke as they try not to sink under my added weight. The one on the right rears up a little, but he's so tiny, it barely moves my arm. I realize I'm kicking my legs, treading air, as if that would somehow help the dragons stay aloft.

I peer down over my feet and see Katya and Smith waving their arms. Lizzie is shouting something, but she's so far down I can't hear her. I have no idea how to make the dragons move lower. Or, really, how to make them move at all.

Katya and Smith are doing this thing with their arms like

the guys at airports do when they're pointing out where the pilots should park the airplanes. The little dragons are snorting smoke and their leathery wings are beating a mile a minute just to keep us up in the air.

"Sorry, tiny dudes," I tell them. "I'm sure it's perfectly acceptable for a gnome to hitch a ride with you guys, but I know this is not the same. If you can just get me over to Glowerton, so I can swoop in and get those maps, I will leave you alone forever."

I don't think they can understand me. Not like the giant dragons in the books understand *their* riders. Ugh. Why is everything so hard? I *know* this place. I *know* these people and these things. Or at least I thought I did.

The dragon on the left is trying to chew on my hand. The one on the right is trying to scratch its face with one of its legs. "Onward, dragon!" I command, just like Custard does in the books.

Nothing.

"Hi-ya!" I yell, and give a little jerk to see if that will get them moving.

Nope.

"Charge!" I yell, giving them both a squeeze with my arms. They don't like that, and each of them sends a stream of fire out of their nostrils to prove it.

"Sorry," I say. Then, to myself, "How do I get these weird things to move?" But just as I say it, a rainbow appears incredibly close to us. The colors are so bright. I've never see anything like it.

"Oh my gosh," I breathe. "What in the . . . ?" The tiny dragons begin flapping furiously toward the colors. The rainbow is just out of our reach, though. "Come on, tiny monsters," I say. "You can do it." It feels like at any moment we could grab a handful of red or orange or yellow or green. My feet smack into tree branches and leaves as we fly closer to the rainbow that is juuuuuust out of our reach. After a few minutes I see little roofs below us. Glowertown! Hey! We're here! And just like that the rainbow disappears and I see him, just above us, wearing a bashed-up green hat and holding a small horn. It's Johnny O'Sprocket, lamest gnome in the books.

Except. Except. He just led my dragons right to their destination when they weren't going to move at all. He distracted me into not being so scared. What the heck? Johnny O'Sprocket is actually *cool*?!

He gives me a salute, smiles brightly, and then bounds off, shooting tiny rainbows as he flies through the air. What a strange little dude.

I'm straining to see anything through the leaves. I see

gnomes wandering along wooden walkways that are strung between the trees, just like Ewoks in *Return of the Jedi*. There are trolls, too, and I worry that the walkways aren't reinforced enough to hold their weight. Some of the trolls are chained together, some of them are chained to trees with longs lengths of links. They are using their bare hands to pull at pieces of bark that hang from the wide tree trunks. Underneath the bark is something flowing, thick and red.

We fly over one huge tree. The trunk is massive, as wide as a school bus. Down through the branches and leaves I see an orange glow. It's a skylight built into a little tree house cabin. Through the skylight I see stacks of maps on a table and three or four gnomes bent over them.

"Bingo," I whisper to myself. Now I have to figure out how to get in there and out. No problem, right? One of the chained trolls outside the cabin lifts his eyes, and he sees me. He makes a startled grunt, which earns him a poke from a gnome who I guess is watching over them. The gnome is holding something that looks like a fireplace poker. Thank goodness, he doesn't look up. He walks along the wooden walkway and around a corner out of sight. The first troll pokes the trolls he's chained to, and they all look up now. They eye me and the dragons, curiously. I wonder why they're all chained like that. They're so big, it seems like the trolls would have the *gnomes* all chained up. But then, those trolls we saw in the woods were chained and taken by gnomes, too. Weird.

The dragons are flapping their wings in a way that I think means they're excited. The one on the left blows smoke from its nose and tries to dive. It doesn't make any progress, though, because its counterpart under my other arm is still trying to scratch its nose. Once its nose is successfully scratched, it catches a whiff of whatever the dragon smelled and wiggles with excitement. The next thing I know, we're diving straight down into the tree. The trolls are chained together but do their best to scatter as we come hurtling toward them. I see the wooden walkway flying up at my face at alarming speed.

"*Ooof,*" I grunt as we crash, the dragons escaping from my clutches and running over to lick oozing red sap from the enormous tree trunk. I'm lying on the walkway, trying to catch my breath, when a gnome comes straight for me with his spear.

"What you think you're doing now, huh? Coming to steal my trolls? That's not likely to happen, even if you are some kind of huge mutant." He aims his spear right at my throat. I throw my arms up in front of me, like that might help, and then, preparing to be stabbed, I feel . . . nothing.

I realize I've slammed my eyes closed, but only after I open them and see that the gnome is not there anymore. A troll is holding him in the air by his shirt collar, and the gnome is writhing and dangling like a fish at the end of a fishing pole. The troll smiles, showing off brown teeth. He uses two fingers to reach into the gnome's tiny shirt pocket, and he pulls out a set of keys. Then he flings the gnome out into the trees like some kind of shot put.

"Oh my g—" My head whips around to see the gnome flying through the air. "You can't just throw people!" There's a distant *"Ahhhhhhhh!"* and a crash. I swallow hard and turn back around to face the troll.

The troll is smiling still. He holds up the end of a broken chain that had attached his ankle to the troll next to him. It sizzles and smokes and he winces, dropping it. The troll next to him is just sitting there on the lightly swaying wooden walkway, looking me up and down.

Did the chain break when the dragons and I crashed into it? It must have. The troll holds the set of keys and kisses them. He unlocks the shackle on his foot and carefully steps away from his broken chain. Then he goes to the other trolls and unlocks their chains as well. Every time the chain touches a troll, it sizzles and smokes and the troll grunts a little. A few gnomes come running around the corner of the large tree trunk, holding long spears, but when they see what's happening, they stop in their tracks. They shout to each other and run away across another walkway.

"I think they're going to get reinforcements," I say to the trolls. "You better get out of here. Well, unless you want a fight on your hands. Maybe you do. I mean, you are a troll. And *trolls are prone to beastly outbursts, unpredictable and dangerous.* That's from book one. Of the Triumphant Gnome Syndicate books?" I should stop talking. But I can't. I don't want this guy to eat me. Though . . . I can tell by the shape of his eyes, the tilt of his head, he doesn't seem to want to eat me. He's just staring at me.

"I'm a human," I say slowly. "Huuuuu maaaaan." I point to my chest.

"You're here because of the prophecy," he says. His voice is as clear and understandable as my dad's. I feel like an idiot for assuming he was an idiot. *Man*, Macinaw. Is anything in the books accurate?

I nod slowly. "Prophecies are kind of stupid, though, don't you think? Like, did my eyes light up or anything when you said that? Did I look excited?"

He shrugs and gives me a funny look. "You look kind of

like you're about to wet your pants, no offense." He clears his throat. "Anyway, I don't have enough experience with prophecies to be able to say if they're stupid or not."

I feel my cheeks redden. "I guess I don't have any experience, either. Just from books I've read and stuff, they seem—"

"We need to go," another troll interrupts. "Right now." Gnomes are running down the walkways, dozens of them, armed with a variety of very sharp-looking weapons. A few of the spears seem to be sparking at their pointy ends. That doesn't look great.

"If you're here for the prophecy," the first troll asks as we all retreat, "why are you *here*, exactly? Don't you need the mace?"

I feel a little weird talking about the mace with this guy. I mean, I'm trying to find it so I can potentially vanquish his queen. Not like I know how I'll do that, but even so. "Well," I say. "I mean, yeah. I'm trying to find the mace. But also, my sister is lost. She left a weird clue and I'm trying to find some maps these gnomes stole." Should I be telling a troll all this? I am a terrible hero. I can't stop myself, though, my mouth just keeps moving. "Do you know where Troll Mountain is?" I look up at him hopefully. The gnomes are closing in, and he pushes me behind him protectively.

"Never heard of it," he says. "That's a really dumb name for a mountain."

The first of the gnomes reaches us. We're all backed up against the huge trunk of a tree, totally surrounded. My heart is trying to leap out of my throat. This is so confusing. I mean, maybe I shouldn't be hiding behind this troll. I should probably just pop out and go over to the gnome side, all, "Hey, my bros, what's up with these super-smart trolls?" but yikes.

"You tree trunks!" one of the gnomes yells. "You putrid bags of fish guts. Who do you think you are? You motherless piles of dung." Another gnome spits at the trolls and smiles, his upper lip curling like a growling dog's. "You bags of hammers. You broken lanterns. There's no light behind your imbecilic eyes, so why do you even try to escape? Get on your knees."

Jeez. These gnomes are so mean. Are there *any* good guys Flipside? Well, other than Johnny O'Sprocket?

"Where are these maps you seek?" the troll asks as he grabs the spear from the first gnome and flings it, a javelin through the sky. Next he picks up the gnome and tosses him after the spear.

"Uh," I say watching the gnome sail over the treetops. "Over there." I point to the cabin built into the branches several yards away. It's at the end of a walkway that isn't connected to ours. The window glows in the dimness of the forest light, and it seems like the cabin is empty. I guess all the gnomes are here trying to insult troll mothers and possibly kill us.

The other trolls seem to be having a blast tossing gnomes into the trees. They're laughing and chatting, barely even paying attention, as if they're yanking weeds out of a garden and talking about the football game last night.

"I can help you, if you want," the troll says. "It's the least I can do, really. I can't thank you enough for breaking my chains. Those terrible goblins sided with the gnomes years ago, and the metal they smelt has some kind of magic in it. It burns us when we touch it. Evil stuff. It makes the trolls timid, scared of the gnomes. How did that ever happen?" The last question doesn't seem to be for me. He gazes off into the distance, in thoughtful silence for a minute. Then he grabs me, his hand pretty much taking up the entire part of my arm above the elbow, and like the Hulk, just leaps over to the next walkway, dragging me along with him.

We burst into the cabin. There's one gnome still at the table, holding a magnifying glass and looking at a map. He glances up at us, startled, then throws the magnifying glass as he jumps to his feet. It hits the troll square in the forehead and bounces off, clattering to the wooden floor.

In two long and fast strides the troll has the gnome by the shirt. He's cocking his arm, ready to throw the gnome through the glass skylight, when I hold out my hand. "How about not throwing this one. Just . . . I mean, you don't have to kill them, do you?"

"Do you think it kills them to throw them?" The troll shrugs. "I never thought about it. They seem really bouncy."

The gnome dangles, spitting and cursing. "You rock-head, you goat for brains. You sniveling piece of stupid—"

"I'm going to throw him."

I sigh. "Okay."

The glass shatters, raining down on us, as the gnome flies out into the sky. I shake glass off the maps, grabbing the stacks and finding a bag on the floor in the back of the room. I stuff as many maps as I can fit in the bag and then toss the bag over my shoulder.

"This is all I can carry," I say. "Let's go find the dragons."

"Dragons?" He laughs. It's a low rumble that builds like thunder. "Let's not." He grabs me, throws me onto his back like a bag of maps, and jumps straight up superhero style, right out the window. Holy cow!

We shoot into the sky, where I can see the sun getting lower. Then we plummet through leaves and branches. It feels like we're moving about a thousand miles an hour. Surely we're going to just smash into the ground. Maybe he can survive with his troll bones, but I'm going to be a big Buck splatter.

We stop plummeting, though, as he flings an arm out and grabs a tree trunk. We swing around the trunk like King Kong, and then he gracefully drops to the floor of the forest with a thump. He reaches back and pulls me gently off his back and sets me down. My legs feel like Jell-O. There are splinters all over me like I'm becoming a porcupine/human mutant.

The troll reaches into a pocket on his tattered pants and hands me a rock. It's sandy-colored and dusty. He puts it in my hand and says, "This is for you." I take the rock even though I'm not sure what to do with it.

I nod and say, "Okay. Um. Thanks."

The troll touches his chest. "Jan."

"Jan?" I say. "Nice to meet you. I'm Buck."

He gives me a broad smile. "Nice to meet you, brother!" He runs off after the other trolls who have leapt from the trees and taken off into the woods.

I guess the trolls didn't throw all the gnomes out of

Glowerton, because there are gnomes in sight now, coming down the trees, looking like swarming termites. I take off running, too, and run right smack into Smith, sending us both sprawling. Katya, Lizzie, and the Healer come up to us.

"Buck! Did you see him? The real Johnny O'Sprocket! He was up there!" Lizzie waves her hand at the tops of the trees and I swear she has actual hearts in her eyes.

"I saw him," I say, breathing hard. "He was awesome. But right now we have to run, run, run!"

So we do.

16

It turns out, when you've been walking through a forest all day, and then you ride some dragons, and then you meet a troll, and then you steal some maps, and then you run for your life when the gnomes want the maps back . . . this is all very tiring. It feels like my right side is about to split open. I really can't run anymore. I'm going to have to just give up and be captured by gnomes. I don't know what else to do. Lizzie and Smith are way far ahead. The Healer is on Smith's back. Katya is just behind them, still a little slowed down by her injuries but WAY faster than me. I'm huffing and puffing and sweating and at any moment my heart is going to explode.

"I can't . . . ," I puff out. "You guys . . ." But I don't

have enough breath to make my words any louder. At least Lizzie took the maps from me. When I'm caught I'll have nothing for the gnomes. I fall to my knees, then to my face, knocking my glasses off. The crunching running behind me gets louder and louder. I close my eyes. It feels so good to stop, I don't care if they get me. I take huge gulps of the cool forest air, lying on my back in the leaves.

"There he is!" someone shouts. "Get hi—" I prepare myself for being grabbed, beaten, torn apart, fed to dragons. But nothing happens. The running sounds stop and there are a lot of shouts. I open my eyes and sit up. There's a scuffle happening not too far away. I squint but can't see anything. There's screaming, then the running crunches in the opposite direction, fading back into the deep woods. I pat the leaves and find my glasses. I get them on my face just when Lizzie arrives, smiling triumphantly. She's holding one of Katya's slingshots.

"I borrowed some soulstinkers from the Healer. Bam bam bam!" She mimes shooting the slingshot. "Those things are impressive." She reaches her hand down and pulls me to a standing position. "You need to buck up, Buck. Come on." She's holding my hand, pulling me toward the rest of the crew.

"Good work," Katya says when we get closer. She pats Lizzie on the butt and smiles. "You follow directions well." Lizzie beams.

"You just let her take on like six gnomes by herself!" I can't believe how mad I am suddenly. "What if they hit her with another mindbomb? What if they—" But I can't even finish that thought. It makes me nauseous. "Are you crazy?!"

"You just rode dragons into an entire town," Katya points out.

"Yeah, but—" I say, then I see the fire in Lizzie's eyes and decide I should stop talking. Because even though I'm mad, and even though it terrifies me what those gnomes could have done to Lizzie if she hadn't been victorious . . . what was I going to say? Yeah, but I'm the hero? Yeah, but I'm the expert? Yeah, but I'm the tough guy? Any of those things would get me smacked in the ear, or worse.

"Now that the coast is hopefully clear for a while, maybe we should look at the maps," I say, trying to take a deep breath and divert the conversation. I keep saying stupid things. But maybe it's because I *think* stupid things? Argh. I don't think stupid things. I just want Lizzie to be safe. She didn't ask to come here. I mean, neither did I, really, but I kind of did, because I've been dreaming about something like this for so long.

That's when it hits me. Lizzie was right. I *don't* think of this as her adventure. I think of it as mine. Is that wrong? I don't know. I dig through the bag, looking for a map that shows the whole of Flipside. I find one and spread it out on the forest floor. It's getting pretty dark, so the Healer flicks a claw and a flame leaps up, lighting the map.

It's like nothing I've ever seen. The legend takes up nearly half of the page. Tunnels and trails, gnome passages, troll roads, rivers, meadows, underground cities, cities in the trees. But no mountains. How can that be? I flip the map over, but there's nothing on the back.

"How can there be NO MOUNTAINS?!" I grab the Healer's flaming claw and hold it closer to the map. The fancy scrolling design on the sides proves that part of the map hasn't been torn off or anything. This really is all of Flipside. I reach in the front pocket of my pants and pull out the folded book cover with the smeared message from Willy.

Troll ~~cl~~ has us

~~in~~ a mountain

Please help

Maybe I misinterpreted it. Maybe the troll doesn't actually have a mountain. Maybe she meant the troll *is* a mountain. Like, it's really big. Ugh. I don't know. Also, that is super–not helpful because yeah, trolls are big.

"Hey," Lizzie says, pointing at the map. "Look." She's pointing to an area where the forest dissolves into desert.

For a minute I'm trying to figure out how what she's pointing at has anything to do with mountains or Willy, but then it hits me. Ooooh. Hmm. *"Master Hob wanted nothing more than peace for all creatures. When he disappeared into the High Desert, he took the Troll Vanquishing Mace with him, and with it he buried the years of hatred,"* I say.

Lizzie taps the map. "Maybe we should go this way."

I don't see any mountains near the desert, which means no Willy near the desert. But I don't see mountains anywhere, so . . . . I sigh.

"What you just said," Smith says, kneeling next to me. "That was from Macinaw's books?"

I nod.

"Unbelievable," Smith mutters. "Well, come on. Let's go. His terrible books all have a twist of the facts in them. Maybe the mace is in the desert after all. Master Hob disappeared along the seashore, but there were quiet rumors that he must have trekked through the desert first, hunting for a place to either hide or destroy the mace. I never believed he would destroy it, though."

I look at the map. The seashore spans the far edge of the desert, about a bajillion miles from here. We'll need the mace to rescue Willy and Macinaw, though, and with no mountains on the map, this is really the only way we can go with any certainty. We all agree to plod ahead.

We can camp on the edge of the desert tonight instead of in the creepy woods. As we walk through the dark forest, I think about my day. I spent most of it running from gnomes, not from trolls. In fact, Jan was super-nice. At least to me he was. It's all very confusing. I roll up the map and put it in the back with the others.

"Don't you want to look at the rest of the maps?" Lizzie asks as I toss the bag over my shoulder.

"Sure," I say. "But we can do that later. We're losing light. We should get moving."

"But what if that map is some old thing, and there's an updated one?" she asks.

Lizzie is starting to drive me crazy with all her questions. It's like she thinks I'm doing everything wrong. "I'm pretty sure that a map is a map is a map," I say. My voice has that grouchy edge to it that happens when I'm tired. "It's not like the desert can be moved to a different place."

Lizzie bites her lip and turns away. She and Katya push

ahead. Smith and the Healer and I are just behind them. Even with the Healer's finger flame, everything is just so dark. It feels like the trees are caving in, trying to grab us. It's getting cold, too.

I shove my hands in my pockets, glad my ratty old cargo shorts haven't been completely torn from my body yet. Between crawling in holes, riding dragons, and falling through trees, they're so dirty Mom would have a heart attack, but they're holding up pretty well. My hand closes around the rock Jan gave me. It's cool and heavy and reminds me of when I was younger and always managed to find a pretty rock to shove in my pocket. It didn't matter if I was at school, or in a parking lot, or at the park, there was always some awesome rock that seemed to just call my name. I pull the rock out and look at it. It's too dark to really see any detail, but it has a little bit of sparkle. Nice.

"Buck."

"Hmm?" I turn to the Healer.

"I didn't say any words," he says, holding the flame up to his face. "Thinking about where to find more tree frings, I am."

"Oh," I say, and look at Smith. He's staring up into the leaves as he walks—how can he do that without falling down? His whip is in his hand like he expects something to jump out at us at any moment.

"I must be hearing things," I mutter to myself. I jog up to Lizzie and Katya, who are only a few yards ahead.

"Think we're close to the desert?" I ask. "Also, anyone have a snack?" I make a face that I hope is cute, and rub my stomach.

"I *wish* I had a snack," Lizzie says. "If we don't find some food soon I might have to eat Katya." Katya shoves her elbow and Lizzie staggers to the side a bit, laughing. At some point Katya removed her bandages. Her clothes are torn from the trolls who attacked her, but I can't really see any gaping wounds. The Healer does amazing work.

Katya and Lizzie are discussing whether Katya's fingers would be the first snack, or her toes, when I drop back. Those two are like best friends now. I guess it's nice, but it makes me itchy. Lizzie is my best friend. And Katya tried to kill me. She's been nicer since then, but still. How can Lizzie be buddy-buddy with her? We're on this adventure together.

I'm back with the Healer and Smith now. The Healer hands me a mushroom.

"This isn't going to kill me, is it?" I joke as I pop it in my mouth.

"Maybe just make your hairs fall out," he says.

I spit the mushroom out as fast as I can—all over the back of Smith's head. He turns slowly and I smile, pieces of mushroom in my teeth. "Sorry," I say. He clenches his jaw, turns his head back around, and wipes his hand down the back of his hair. I hope the spit-out pieces won't make *his* hair fall out.

So much for my snack hunt.

After what feels like a thousand more hours, Katya says, "This will do," and stops walking. I guess we've found our campsite for the night. The trees are growing sparse now and there's plenty of space to stretch out on the ground and sleep. I'm so tired I don't care that there isn't a lot of cover and we could be discovered by angry gnomes and trolls. I just want to curl in a ball and sleep for a week. We gather leaves to try to make soft pallets for sleeping, but it doesn't really matter to me. The ground itself feels like the nicest mattress in the world. My eyes are closed, my thoughts fading before I even realize that Lizzie is sleeping next to Katya instead of me.

I wake up and my mouth is so dry I gag. Well, that's lovely. I don't remember Han Solo ever gagging from lack of food and water. I can't recall one time that Harry Potter couldn't pee because he hadn't had liquid in his body for hours upon hours. I have lost all concept of time. All I know is that I can't swallow because my tongue is a dried-up lump of flesh, and that the sun is up, and that Lizzie and Katya and Smith and the Healer don't seem to be a gagging disgusting mess like I am.

I think I was dreaming about the Fake Buck and Fake Willy and Fake Lizzie back at home. I had kind of forgotten about them, but now I can't help but wonder . . . what the heck are they doing there? Are Mom and Dad still in that scary sleep? Maybe Mom and Dad have woken up and they're being fooled by all the fake kids. Oh, no! What if Fake Buck is ruining my high score on the Triumphant Gnome Syndicate game?! What if he's failing all the pop quizzes at school?! Man. There's just so much happening, and I can't seem to fix anything.

Smith is looking at the big map, the one that shows all of Flipside. I have no idea how we're going to make it to Troll Nest. It's going to be days of walking. We're going to die of dehydration and starvation before we get there, even with the bursts of wind Katya has been using to give us a little boost every now and then. She's still weak, though, and can't keep it up. There are too many of us.

Smith rolls up the map and puts it back in the bag.

"According to hearsay, Hob was seen near the old Weeping Hedge. I don't think it's far from here. Come on." We all start walking. There isn't really much to say. We've officially passed the edge of the forest. There's no sign of the mace. There's no sign of *anything*. The trees are nearly gone now, the ground basically desert, but rockier than you would think. Lizzie and Katya have fallen back behind us, with Smith and me taking the lead now. The Healer keeps bouncing between us all, trying to get us to eat things that *"maybe won't kill you, but maybe will kill your pancreas."* I have avoided maybe killing my pancreas so far, though I'm not sure if I can last much longer. These are things he collected in the forest. I doubt there's going to be anything to eat in a desert. I might have to give in and eat some of this stuff he—literally—dug up. Where's a witch offering some Turkish Delight when you need her?

The sky goes on forever and the sun is killer bright. It's nice to feel the warmth after having been in the forest for so long, but I know it's going to get hot soon. It smells musty out here, like when you're playing kickball in the part of the park where all the grass has been trampled and it's just dirt. Or, you know, if you're watching everyone else play kickball because you haven't been chosen for any team but your mom made you go outside anyway because "six consecutive hours on a screen is going to make your brain melt out of your ears, Buck."

"This doesn't really look like a place where there would be a hedge," I say to Smith. "Even a weeping one."

"The Weeping Hedge doesn't really exist anymore," he says. "It's a thing of history. But there are vines and stumps that gnomes say once belonged to the hedge."

I shrug. Whatever. At this point, I will take any far-fetched clue or direction we can get. I pick up a rock to look at it. It says, "Hey, it's you."

I stop in my tracks and Lizzie crashes into me.

"What the heck, Buck?" she says, staggering back and rubbing her nose.

I hold up the rock. "I think that rock just said hi. Did you hear it?"

"Haha, very funny. Come on." Lizzie pushes past me.

"For real!" I shout after her. "It said, 'Hey, it's you.'" I toss the rock to the ground and it yells, "Not cool, dude!"

"What is saying this thing to you?" the Healer asks when he catches up.

"That rock," I say, pointing. "Maybe it's starvation or something, but I swear it talked to me. Did you hear it?"

The Healer shakes his head, his mouth in a tight frown.

I lean over and before I can pick up another rock it says, "She's looking for you."

"See!" I shout. "Did you hear that!" I know how crazy it sounds, but it's true. They really seem to be talking to me. But no one else can hear them? I start laughing like that guy who has all his earthly possessions in a shopping cart and hangs out by the gas station. The one Dad gives five dollars to every time we see him.

The Healer tilts his head to the side and says, "You talk to the rocks."

"No," I say. "The rocks talk to me!"

"I mean, please for you to say something to the rocks." He motions to the ground and looks at me with wide eyes. By this time, Lizzie and Katya have caught up to see what all the commotion is about. Smith is standing off to the side, his arms crossed over his chest.

"Okay," I say. "Um. Hey there, rocks. Know a good place a guy can find a drink of water?" I should feel ridiculous, I know, but I'm so thirsty and hungry and tired, and so many weird things have already happened, that this just seems like regular everyday weirdness at this point.

"Rocks?" I say. "Did you hear me?"

Lizzie starts to giggle. She's just as punchy as I am.

"Fourteen steps to your left. One step forward. Three steps to the right. One foot down." The voices are all different, but they make complete sentences. They echo in my brain like my own thoughts, but somehow . . . louder. I'm scrambling around, repeating to the group what the rocks are saying to me.

I count out the steps, kneel, and start digging with my hands. "This is crazy," I say. "I must be officially, clinically nuts from the hunger and the dehydration." There isn't anything in the sand except sand. Until . . .

"What's this?" I feel something like a rope in the sand. I tug on it and wipe the sand from it. It looks like a rope, too. I feel like the craziest person who ever crazied. "Not water," I say, standing and wiping the sand off my hands. "I am a nutbar for real now."

The Healer dances around my feet like Rumpelstiltskin. He drops to his knees and yanks at the rope, hard. One end pops out of the ground and sprays me right in the face with a stream of water. I splutter and choke and then yell, "WHAT?"

"Water root!" the Healer yells. "A mystery of mysteries how it grows or where you find it, but here it is. Water root! Water root!"

We all take turns drinking and when it seems like there's

enough water, we soak our shirts in it and let it run through our hair.

"Do you know what this means?" Lizzie says, grabbing me by both gloriously wet shoulders.

"That we aren't going to die? At least not today?" I laugh and shake my wet hair in her face.

"No, no, dummy! Well, yes . . . but no! It means you're a rockmouth, Buck. A rockmouth!"

Whoa. I put my hands on my head. "I heard the rocks talk," I say. "And then I talked to the rocks. Chapter fourteen in book three. *Custard was jealous of the network of rockmouths, but knew he'd need their help in the coming months.* Why didn't I remember?"

"Maybe because you've only read it once," Lizzie says.

"A rockmouth," I say. "That's really rare. It's something only a few gnomes have ever been able to—"

"You're not a gnome," Smith says. It's the first time he's spoken in a while. His face is pinched, like he just sucked on a lemon instead of water root.

"But he's a rockmouth," the Healer says. "That is for sure, for sure."

"So what does it mean?" I ask. I trip on a dead plant and go sprawling. It's hard to walk and talk and be excited at the same time.

"It means . . . ," Smith says, but his voice trails off.

My mouth is full of sand. Gross. I'm spluttering and spitting while everyone just stares at me. Yes, yes, Buck the Clumsy. Fine, but why do they have to stare. And point? Lizzie is pointing at me now, her mouth hanging open. Surely it's not THAT much of a surprise that I would spontaneously face-plant. I stand up and brush the sand off me as best I can. Everyone is quiet.

"What?" I say. "Make a guy feel *more* self-conscious, would you."

"Buck," Lizzie says, still pointing. "BUCK." She blinks and blinks.

I finally look where she's pointing. What in Hob's pants?! It wasn't a dead plant I tripped on, it was a wooden handle with intricate carvings. Could it be? I drop to my knees and dig at the sand around the handle, loosening it until I can yank it from the ground. Holy cow. No way. *No way!* Finally, something convenient and crazy and totally unbelievable has happened—just like in a book. I *tripped* on the Troll Vanquishing Mace?! Hahaha! What!

17

I swing the Troll Vanquishing Mace through the air, and everyone jumps back a foot. I guess I'd do that, too, if I saw me brandishing this thing. Even if it's only for trolls, it still wouldn't feel great to get whacked in the head with it. Though it's not nearly as big as I thought it would be.

"Good work, team!" I shout, flinging the mace around. "Between the map and the books, we just walked right into this thing, no Weeping Hedge necessary! Bam!"

Lizzie's squinting and she's glancing all around. "You don't think this was a little too easy?" she asks.

"What?" I say, slashing the air. "No way. This was all skill."

Katya's arms are crossed over her chest. She seems a little skeptical, too.

"Come on, you guys," I say. "Everything doesn't have to be hard, you know? We should be thankful this was so easy."

Smith takes a deep breath and looks at Katya. She just barely shrugs and looks at me; then she scans the horizon. I'm not sure anyone believes this is actually the mace. It feels sturdy in my hands, though, like it was meant to be there. And the carvings . . . it's the Battle of the Trolls from Before Time Started. This is definitely the mace.

"Okay, then, good work, Buck. Now drop it." Smith's eyes are like steel, his hand motioning for me to drop the mace. But I don't want to put it down just yet. I mean, this has been a long journey. I'd like to take a minute to check out my booty.

You know what I mean.

"Man," I say, moving away from Smith. "Look at this thing."

"Put it down so I can see it more closely. I need to make sure it's what we're looking for," Smith snaps at me, but I hold the mace higher and step farther away from him.

"Just *wait* a second, will you?" I thought it would be bigger, honestly. The wooden stick is short, but the hilt is huge. My hand could be twice its size, maybe even three times its size, to wrap around the scummy, cracking brown leather that twists around the grip. I pick a rotten chunk of leather off the hilt and drop it to the ground. "Kinda looks like your face," I say to the Healer with a wink. He punches me in the stomach way harder than he needs to. I give an *oof* and double over for a second.

Smith puts his hands on his hips. "Stop fooling around, and *drop the mace.*"

"Just be patient," I gasp, giving a weak but exasperated look at the Healer, who is now smiling brightly at me. "I want to look at it for a minute. Jeez, Smith." I spin away from him. Lizzie comes closer to inspect it. The hilt is huge and the stick part is short and the round, spiky mace seems too small to inflict any major damage on a troll. I guess it's the magic that does most of the damage. If it's anything like in the book or the game, it'll send a troll flying back a hundred feet with one small tap. I wish there was a troll around to test it on.

"What's this for?" Lizzie pokes at the rusty chain hanging off the end of the hilt. I can't believe she doesn't remember.

"I can't believe you don't remember!" I wrap the chain around my hand and swing the mace around my head like a lasso. "Custard loses his whip in book two? Has to take out some trolls by the sea? Hob makes sure the mace is waiting for him. He hammers the chain into the hilt so he can fling it around like his whip and he lays waste to, like, a million trolls."

"That was the Troll Vanquishing Mace?" Lizzie makes a face. "I guess so, I thought—"

"Oh, for Hob's sake, GIVE THAT TO ME!" Smith, obviously tired of our chatting and inspecting, lunges at me with his Not-a-Whip Chopstick. He's trying to knock the mace from my grip. I whip the mace around the top of my head and laugh. It's not like I want to play Monkey in the Middle with Smith, he's just being so serious and boring. We found the mace! Why can't he take one second to enjoy it! This is the culmination of the first part of our journey. If we were in a book, it would mean the big battle was nigh, it'd mean we'd hit the part with the celebration before having to walk across lava to fight the dragon or fly our ship around the edges of a black hole to get to the forbidden planet. This is the moment we get to take a deep breath. This is the moment we get to—

"Hey!" I yell. Smith pushes me hard. It throws me off-balance and my arm goes down in a flash, because the chain is still wrapped around my hand. The mace slams into the sand and I pull my hand back fast. Something flutters from the hilt of the mace. I quickstep away from Smith and grab a tiny scroll off the ground by my feet. The paper is so old it cracks and crumbles as I try to unroll it. . . . *master of the mace.* That's the only line I can make out. The rest is rolled up and turning to dust. So . . . wait. Could this little scroll be part of the Scrolls of Gnomekind? I squinch up my nose and hold the crusty paper closer to my face, but Smith yanks the paper from me and shoves it in his pocket.

"No more games, little boy. Give it to me."

Why is he being such a jerk about this? It's not the One Ring, though it sure seems to be having a similar effect on him.

"Fine," I say, exasperated. "Take your precious." I do my best Gollum impression and drop the weapon. "You're going to have to let me practice with it, though. I'm going to need lessons or something."

Lizzie glances at me. She doesn't roll her eyes. I wonder if she wants to.

Smith lashes the mace to his back and doesn't say another word.

"Do you think I'm the answer to the prophecy or not?" I ask.

This time Lizzie does roll her eyes.

Smith puts his hand on his hip and stares at me.

"What?!" I say. "Is there something in my teeth? Why aren't you answering? If you think I'm this fancy person, or whatever . . . this guy who's going to *restore balance as the bruising fates bring about a new day*, then I'm going to need some practice. I can't restore balance as a clumsy kid. I need a training montage."

"Okay, okay, you need to quiet down," Katya says. "Your training will come soon enough." She motions for us all to sit in the sand. "Now that we have the mace, let's make sure we're taking the shortest route to Troll Nest. Not that roaming a desert isn't enticing"—she uses the back of her hand to wipe sweaty sand off her face—"but just in case there's an alternate route . . ." I pull the bag off my back. Katya takes out the maps and lays them in the sand. They're all kind of wet. Oops. Actually, more than kind of wet. Most of them are soaked.

"Oh, no," Lizzie breathes. "This is not good."

Smith looks like he's ready to murder me on the spot.

The ink is running, like it's melting and dissolving. Oh, crud. Oh, crud, oh, crud, oh—hey. Wait a second.

"Let me see that," I say, dropping to my knees and leaning over the big map of Flipside. It's not that the ink is spreading out, it's that it's faded a bit and there are new lines appearing, like when you do that thing with lemon juice and an iron. The secret message thing.

There are a bunch of jaggedy lines that I thought were just branches of the ink that smeared, but no. I think it's writing. And whoa, WHOA, all along the top edge of the map, just past the desert, mountains are appearing.

"Is this right?" I scramble to my feet, feeling electricity flow through my body. "There are mountains at the end of the desert? Why didn't you say something?"

Smith and Katya exchange a look. "There are no mountains, Buck," Smith says slowly. "Not for tens of thousands of years."

"What? But look. What is this? What *are* these maps?"

Smith shrugs. "Ancient artifacts? Believe me, if there were mountains, we'd know. Flipside belongs to the gnomes, Buck. We know every inch of our world."

The Healer is hopping from foot to foot like he has to go to the bathroom. "These maps are special kinds of maps. These are troll maps."

No one says anything, because it seems kind of, I don't know . . . ridiculous? Everyone knows that trolls can't read or write. They're basically blue gorillas with (not much) less hair. Well, I guess except for Jan. He was pretty smart for a gorilla-type creature.

The Healer points to the map. "Troll magic this is."

I put my hands up like he just shot a fireball in my face. "Wait, wait, wait," I say. "Troll magic? Trolls don't have magic."

"I can't believe I'm saying this," Smith says, "but I have to agree with Buck."

"YES. HIGH FIVE." He leaves me hanging.

"There's no such thing as troll magic, Healer," Smith says, his voice low and serious. "Trolls are lowly beasts. It is this way now, as it has always been."

I get a shiver. Smith sounds formal, like the gnomes in the books.

"Much you do not know," the Healer says, sounding a lot like Yoda. He shakes his head. "You gnomes, you think you've always been the leader ones, but not always. Not all the times. I have many ages, you know. Many more than any gnomey gnome. I remember the days of these times." He runs his hand over the map. "Yes. I remember these days."

"Why didn't you say anything about the mountains?" I ask.

"You said a mountain named Troll Mountain," he answers plaintively. "That is not a thing. Never there was a Troll Mountain."

I have so many questions. And my chest is filling, expanding, exploding with hope. Mountains! That has to be where Willy is. Except . . . I sigh as I look at the map. The mountains are on the other side of the desert, opposite of the way to Troll Nest.

"No mountains in Troll Nest?" I ask.

The Healer shakes his head. "Never been."

"Heads up," Katya says, and my heart jumps into my throat. She's pointing. It looks like the glint on the horizon is just a mirage. But when it shines again I know it must be real. I hold my hand up to shade my eyes and I see the glint is joined by others. They're moving closer and at a fast clip, too.

"What is that?" I ask.

"Are we saved?" Lizzie asks. "We can hitch a ride out of this desert? Find some lunch? Then find the mountains?" But by now I think we all know to be wary of such luck.

Clouds of sand obscure everything but the glints; the shining is getting brighter and closer.

"I think they're on horses," I say. "Can that be possible?" As the glints get closer and bigger, I can tell that yes, they're on horses, and there are a lot more than I originally thought. Four of the glints have broken loose from the pack and are moving faaaaaast.

We barely have time to roll up the maps and get them back in their bag before four trolls on horseback race right up to us. Those are the biggest horses I have ever seen. I mean, if you put a horse on the back of another horse, maybe it would only be a few inches smaller than these monsters.

The trolls leap from their horses, smelling like rotten hot dogs and hollering like their hair is on fire.

My chance to be a hero is finally here! A little voice in the back of my head is telling me that maybe I shouldn't try to be brave, maybe something strange is afoot, but I ignore it. Maybe also it is time for BUCK ROGERS TO SHINE LIKE THE HERO HE IS. My heart ratchets into light speed as I rip the mace from Smith's back and whip it over my head, conjuring every battle scene I've played in the massive multiplayer online game. I think of every battle scene in the books. I do my best to be the Custard I know, not the Custard who's been grouchy and angry this whole journey.

The bigger of the two trolls has his sights on Lizzie and I charge toward him, swinging the mace like a crazy person. It connects squarely with his big blue belly and . . . bounces off. He doesn't even feel it, just keeps plodding toward Lizzie, who expertly sticks her foot out and trips him, sending him sprawling.

"What the heck," I mutter. "Do I have to turn it on or

something?" I run back up to the troll, who has already leapt back up to his feet, and I swing the mace, and again it bounces harmlessly off his body. He's not even annoyed by it, he just keeps moving. "Smith!" I yell. "Why isn't it working?! Do I have to say a spell or something?"

Smith is busy flicking his whip at a couple of trolls coming at him. Katya runs to him and sends a burst of air at them, but she's still weak and the trolls are huge. The wind only ruffles their greasy hair. Smith's whip drops one of the trolls to her knees, but the other keeps charging.

The trolls are huge brutes, with snarling faces, and smoking wrists where long chains bind their arms. They seem to be moving pretty well with those chains, though.

There's more dust in the distance, and a loud noise. I can't quite place it, like a car horn but deeper and longer.

"Maori," Katya breathes. "We're in it now." The trolls are encircling us, doing a fantastic job of being one hundred percent unfazed by our attempts at fighting back.

"Maori," I say, feeling relief. "Oh, good. That magical fishhook is about to come in very handy. That thing is so cool. Have you seen him take it and capture whole hordes of trolls?"

"He's about to capture a whole horde of wanted fugitives," Smith says.

I realize Smith is talking about us. "Why would Maori capture *us*? He's your best friend. You've been waging battles since you were *wee lads upon the prairies of Flipside*."

"Maori and I haven't spoken in years," Smith says. "He's a nasty brute."

"*That's* the magical fishing hook?" I say. Maori is holding a weapon that looks like a spiked ball on a very long rope. "You couldn't catch one fish with that thing."

"Maori doesn't go fishing for marine life," Katya says. "Not for a very long time now."

A bright silver glint flies through the sky, landing a few feet from Smith. Soon after, a gnome lands next to it. How did he do that? The gnome is small and dark, his face painted with swirls of black.

"Maori," I breathe.

"I went out for some fishing and look what I discover at the end of my hook." He's eyeing me and Lizzie as he slowly swings the giant hook thing.

"This is none of your concern," Smith says. There's an edge to his voice I've never heard before, and I have heard a *lot* of edges to his voice.

"It sure *looks* like my concern," Maori says, his voice calm but laced with menace. "It looks like the Syndicate's concern, too." Maori steps up to Smith, standing way too close. "Hello, Smith." He curls his lips into a snarl. "Look at you, in the company of Katya the Hermit." He tuts like a grandma. "Seems the meddling sheriff has got himself into a bit of a bind."

Maori steps away from Smith and takes a step closer to me. I shut my mouth, taking an involuntary step back. This guy isn't like the Maori in the books at all. The tattooed swirls and dots on his face are terrifying. He licks his teeth one by one while he looks me up and down. Then he looks at Lizzie in a way that makes me want to punch his face off. I hope Willy never has to see him in real life. Ever.

Maori pulls a small, grubby shell from his pocket and blows into it. The sound that blares out is so loud I can't believe it came from such a tiny thing.

"The Conch of the Syndicate," I whisper. It's so much smaller and uglier than I imagined.

"Yes," Maori answers simply. "I arrest you on behalf of the Syndicate, for trespassing, stealing, consorting with known enemies, criminal intent, and probably a hundred other things."

"We're on a rescue mission," I say. "We're here to find my sister. To find Harold Macinaw."

Maori ignores me. With a flick of his wrist, he has all of us trussed up in the rope of his "fishing" line, which causes us all to fall together in one big lump. "Back to your horses!" he yells at the trolls, and they saunter off. He never takes his eyes off us.

A horse trots over at his command, and with one more flick of Maori's wrist, the fishhook attaches to a silver harness on the back of the horse. He spins his hand in the air, like an orchestra conductor, and the rope tightens around us. We're all squished and on top of each other in the sand, struggling to stand up. Maori yells for us to be still (which we ignore). He produces even more rope and manages to bind Katya's hands so that her palms are facing each other. He reaches into Smith's pocket and takes the small whip. He pulls the mace out of my hands and twirls it like a baton. He binds the rest of our hands, so that now we're not just tied together, we're trussed up good.

"Still chasing fairy tales, I see," he sneers. He stops twirling the mace and looks it up and down. "*This* is the mace? It's more like a rotting toy."

"If it's such a disgrace, give it back. I'll keep watch over the rotting toy," Smith says.

"How did you find this thing, anyway?" Maori asks. "Dumb luck?"

"How about skill and foresight," I retort, surprised to hear my voice out loud. I thought I just said that in my head.

In one step Maori is in my face. His breath reeks to the point where I think he might actually be talking out of his rear end. But no, that would smell better. I wrinkle up my nose and try to breathe through my mouth.

"It was that unicorn, wasn't it?" Maori gives a hearty laugh. "That old thing is garbage, Smith. It was garbage when the gnomes stole it from the trolls and it's garbage now. You know it is. Everyone knows it is. That's why it sits deep under the earth rusting to dust. It's meaningless. Trash."

"Well, that's your opinion. I happen to think it's still very useful."

"You've broken how many laws because you think a fabricated, fake-magic hunk of junk that used to belong to idiot hammerbrains . . . you think that meaningless *garbage* is useful?!"

"Actually, the magic of the trolls is not of the fake kind," the Healer says. "It is, in true fact, older than gnome magic."

Maori snaps his fingers and a troll puts his whole hand over the Healer's face to make him stop talking.

Maori points at Smith. "You're pathetic."

Smith and I haven't become the best of friends on this journey, but it's making my head buzz to hear the way Maori talks to him. My fists clench at my side, though it makes no difference when they're bound like this.

"Your trials will begin as soon as we've assembled witnesses." Maori snaps again and the troll releases the Healer's mouth. Maori saunters off, the troll right behind him, jumps onto his horse, and gallops to the head of the column of horses and trolls. From there, we're dragged along behind the horse we're tied to until I think we're all going to die of sand suffocation.

It's just as the sun is going down that our beleaguered party feels the sand and rocks underneath us turn to scrub and then to grass. The horses stop and gather around a wooden trapdoor in the ground. Maori dismounts and, keeping us all tied together, unlocks the fishhook from the back of the contraption on the horse. He kicks open the trapdoor and before any of us can say one word he pushes us down into the hole.

With a big *oof,* the ball of humans, gnomes, and Healer lands with a squelch.

"Come on, then," a deep voice says, dragging us to our feet. Someone cuts the rope and releases us, but before we can run, each of us is grabbed and shackled.

Goblins. Of course. Working in the dungeons. Weaknesses: running slowly. Strengths: well, strength. The one holding me gives my arm a squeeze. Its oily green hand is slick against my skin.

They split us up, taking the Healer off in a different direction. Lizzie, Smith, Katya, and I are thrust into a nearly pitch-black cell at the end of a long hallway. The only light is from a crackling torch on the wall.

The iron bars clang shut behind us and I immediately think it's interesting how, when you read about a dungeon, you can really feel the dankness, the dark, the cold. But one thing you can't notice when reading about dungeons is the smell. As a brand-new resident of a dungeon, I can say with one hundred percent authority that the smell is . . . what is the equivalent of deafening to a nose? Because it's that. The sewer smell in here seems to be alive—and angry—coming at us with fingers of stench that pluck away at our nose hairs and eyeballs.

My mind won't stop racing, which helps distract me from the smell. I can't stop thinking, Now what? And, How will I find Willy? And, At least it's cooler here than the desert. And, What was the deal with the rockmouth stuff? And, Trials of Epic Importance are serious things. We might really be in trouble.

Then my brain goes completely blank. "Holy whoa," I stammer, because up against the far wall, in chains that are attached to the stone just above his head, is Harold Macinaw.

Macinaw is still wearing the costume clothes from the book release, but they're tattered and dirty. His eyes are closed. It's too dark to see if he's breathing, but his hands are clenched in fists. That doesn't seem like a very dead guy thing to do.

"Hello, traitor," Katya says, marching up to him.

"Katya?" Macinaw says, squinting. His voice sounds faint and rusty. "I'm sorry, they've smashed my glasses. I can barely see two feet in front of me."

"Yes, it's me. I've had a lovely couple of days, thanks to you." She rubs her bloody bandages. "And thanks to this idiot."

Smith walks over to Macinaw and winces as Katya

kicks him in the leg. "Harold," he says, nodding.

"Ah, Sheriff Smith. How nice to see you. Or almost see you, as it were." The old man smiles. "Our plan didn't quite turn out the way we expected, eh?"

Smith shrugs. "It's taking some interesting paths, but I wouldn't call it a failure just yet."

I stand on my tiptoes to inspect Macinaw's chains. If I had a hacksaw I could probably get through them. In a hundred years. Wait. Did Macinaw just say "our plan"?

"And who do we have here?" Macinaw asks, squinting in my direction.

Everything else melts from my brain as Macinaw's eyes meet mine. I can't believe it's really him. THE Harold Macinaw. Even in the middle of a dungeon cell, my heart does great leaps in my chest.

"My—my name is Buck, sir," I stammer. "I'm your biggest fan. I've read your books so many times, I've lost count. I had no idea everything was based on . . . on . . . this." I wave my arms out to my side. "I'm honored to be on this quest to save you, sir. And as soon as we escape I promise I'll use all of my . . . uh . . . powers or whatever to vanquish every troll in sight. We'll have to find my sister first, but then . . ." I do some ninja moves with an invisible mace.

"Buck loves your books," Lizzie says, stepping in, possibly saving me from embarrassing myself to death. "He has them all memorized. Every word."

"And what about you?" Macinaw asks, giving Lizzie an appraising look.

"Oh, I love them, too," Lizzie says, nodding. "Don't get me wrong. But there's this obsession Buck has. I don't know if I've ever felt like that about *anything*."

We're all quiet after that, lost in our own thoughts, I guess, until Macinaw says in a soft voice, "It's always nice to meet my fans. Though I prefer it to happen under different circumstances." He offers up a small smile. His eyes are smart and twinkly, even in this awful place. There's something else in them, though. Something I can't quite place. Kind of like how the Academy was a lot like the books and yet *felt* so different.

I'm not sure what the word "shrewd" means; it sounds like some kind of animal with big teeth. But Mom uses that word to describe the woman who will never give us a discount at the farmers' market. Macinaw's eyes have that same kind of look.

"Have you seen any human kids?" I ask. "Particularly one who's about this tall." I hold my hand up to my chest. "With brown hair, and probably chewing on her fingernails?"

"Human children? Flipside?" Macinaw's face crinkles up. "I don't understand."

"We saw them all disappearing into a Dumpster Topside," I say. "It was the day after you disappeared. My sister was one of the kids in the long line. Heck, Lizzie and I were almost in the line until Smith was able to anticurse us."

Macinaw looks at Smith. "And you don't know where these children were going?"

"I'll give you three guesses, and the first two don't count," Smith says.

Macinaw frowns. "It's a bold play."

Smith says, "These are bold times. Though it doesn't matter how bold she is, we have what we need."

"So how are you getting me out of here?" Macinaw asks. "And our prize over here?" He winks at me. "What's the plan?"

"Getting thrown into a dungeon was never part of the plan, obviously," Smith says. "We'll think of something."

Macinaw's smile gets bigger, but his eyes narrow. "Yes, young man, you *will* think of something. Imagine my surprise to find myself down here in the first place. Would you like to explain how that happened?"

Smith swallows hard. "The Syndicate isn't as . . . convinced . . . as we are that the prophecy is true. When

I implored them to throw support behind our plan, they turned on me. I found myself on my own, going rogue. The plan was for the two of us to take on this task together, but they got to you first." He hangs his head. "I'm sorry about that." When he looks up, his eyes are huge. I've never seen Smith look so vulnerable. He almost looks . . . nice. He tries for a small smile. "I found you, though."

"Fat lot of good THAT does me!" Macinaw yells, his face reddening. Whoa. He's really mad. "We're *all* headed to trial, you imbecile. Most likely sentenced to death. This is not how *my* story is supposed to end."

Lizzie puts her hand on my elbow and pulls me into a corner. "I'm getting a weird feeling," she says. "Like really weird. Like bad weird. Can you figure out what's going on?"

I shrug. "Not really. But Macinaw's not a bad guy, right? Look at him."

Macinaw and Smith are talking quietly now. Macinaw smiles and he looks more like Maori in this moment than the kindly old gnome grandfather I saw when I first got thrown into this dungeon. You know how when the Grinch smiles and his eyebrows unfurl and kind of look like devil horns? If Macinaw had devil horn eyebrows they'd be unfurling right now.

I look at Lizzie and she raises her eyebrows. "Well," I say, swallowing hard. "I mean, some people just have a weird look about them. It doesn't mean they're evil or anything. How could Macinaw be evil? He writes the best books in the world. Custard is a well-rounded hero. He keeps Flipside safe for all creatures. He is constantly destroying trolls without even breaking a sweat. Good guy all around."

Lizzie doesn't look convinced.

"What are you trolls talking about?" Katya drags her chains over and sits at our feet. Lizzie and I sit next to her.

"Macinaw seems a little . . . ," Lizzie whispers, and she bares her teeth, indicating she thinks Macinaw is a badger or a very scary smiling clown.

"Oh, you don't know the half of it," Katya whispers. She doesn't say anything else, though, because Smith walks over.

"What's going on over here? Little powwow?" He's looking at us hard.

I am getting the distinct feeling that something has changed. I can't quite figure it out, but something is definitely different now. Maybe it's just that everyone is feeling tense because we're in a dungeon. Certainly that wouldn't be an unheard-of response. Right?

My gut is trying to tell me something, but I don't want to

listen to my gut right now. I want to believe what I want to believe. I am Fox Mulder. I am Frodo. I am Captain Kirk. I am Harry Potter. I am not a stupid hero who is about to be betrayed by one of his crew. I am not a red shirt about to be killed. I look down at my shirt and my stomach drops.

"So you and Macinaw are friends, huh?" I say, trying to keep it casual. "You didn't really mention that before."

"Why else do you think I wanted you to help me find him?" Smith asks. His words are slow. It's like we're playing chess, but with words.

I bite the inside of my cheek, thinking carefully about what to say next. "But didn't you say someone had taken him? I thought you wanted my help because there's something special about me. I thought we were trying to save the world. Your world. And that Macinaw is somehow involved in helping keep your world together."

"Smart boy," Macinaw says from across the dungeon. Hang on, has he been able to hear everything we've been saying over here? "You've said it in a nutshell, boy. You are here to ensure that the gnome way of life stays strong. Dominant. You're here because the prophecy says we need your help."

My nose crinkles in confusion. "But Maori, and those other gnomes, they think you guys are nuts, huh?"

"They prefer to keep humans out of Flipside business."

"And they prefer that Flipside politics not be sold as mass market entertainment to humans," Katya says, getting up and walking closer to Macinaw and literally looking down her nose at him. "Can't say I blame them on that one."

"They'll be fine once we see the prophecy fulfilled," Smith says. "In fact, we may receive an official apology. These old gnomes, they don't like to go out on a limb. Always want to plod along, never taking a creative approach. It's tiresome. And these days? These days it's dangerous. The trolls are not as stupid as the Syndicate thinks."

"Well, I don't know about that," Macinaw says. "If you put all the trolls together, the whole lot of them, I bet you wouldn't find as many brain cells as that mouse has over there." He flicks his hand at a mouse lying on the stone floor, rigid in death. "They're simple creatures. They need masters. Without gnomes to tell them what to do, they'd spend their days fighting and lazing about. Gnome rule is what gives them purpose. We are the spark they need to survive. They'd just be animals otherwise."

I think about Jan and squeeze the rock in my pocket. He didn't seem like an animal to me. And those other trolls who were with him didn't seem very happy under gnome control. In fact, *none* of the trolls I've met have been all that bad. My brain does a thing like you see in movies, a flashback reel of all my encounters with trolls since I've been Flipside. The only time they were aggressive was when they were with Maori. But even then, if they'd wanted to squish me they could have, but they didn't. It was Maori controlling them. I mean, their legs were chained, for goodness' sake.

So many things in Macinaw's books have been different than in real life, but maybe nothing more dramatically than the trolls. I get this sinking feeling in my belly and my fingertips turn icy. Nausea rises up in me, but I push it back down. Am I on the wrong side of this fight? I take a deep breath. No. There's no way. The trolls have Willy. Would good guys steal all those kids? Put creepy changelings in their places? Freeze all the adults in some kind of endless sleep? No way. No way. No way. I didn't even think trolls were capable of anything like that. They're simple. They have no magic. Except . . . what about the maps and that ink? What did the Healer say about ancient troll magic?

"Maybe the trolls are evolving," I say, with a yawn. "Maybe some of them are smarter than the others. The ones I've met haven't seemed very dumb to me."

Macinaw looks at me with a steady gaze. It's hard for me to read his expression.

"Maybe we should all try to get some rest," Smith says, rubbing his hand over his face. "We aren't going to solve all the problems of Flipside right now." Lizzie and Katya seem to be dozing already.

I have so many questions my brain just kind of shuts down, stuck in an endless loop of *I don't know, I don't know, I don't know.* Eventually I fall into a restless sleep, until there's a clang down the hall from us, and quick footsteps. A goblin, in chain mail and with terrible, dripping skin, clanks open the cell door. "They're ready for you," he says in a voice that sounds like a rusted car door opening for the first time in fifty years.

We file out of the cell and shuffle down the dark hall, our hands and feet shackled. The shackles were made for smaller wrists than mine, so they pinch and cut into my skin. I put my hands in my tattered pockets and I squeeze the rock. Blood is dripping down one of my shackled wrists, and I have a sudden grateful feeling when I remember that Mom forced me to get a tetanus shot last year when I scraped my finger trying to take the old hard drive out of my computer.

The torches throw shadows on the wall that dance to the clinks and clanks of our chains. At the end of the hallway, a doorway leads into a small, empty room with a round iron door. The goblin raps on it twice and it opens from the inside.

Ten gnomes sit in two tiered rows. The ceiling soars above us, with sunlight streaming in from a pyramid-shaped skylight. Five chairs are placed in the spot where the sun shines. The goblin gestures for us to sit down.

"A Trial of Epic Importance, Day 1749 of this year of the Peace, shall henceforth commence," a voice booms down. A gnome from the center of the first row stands. His beard is white and falls almost to his feet. He looks alarmingly like Master Hob, or how I've always imagined Master Hob, at least. I look to see if he has bulging pockets, but he's wearing a robe over his clothes.

"Buck of the Rogers, Lizzie of the Adams, Harold Macinaw of the Eastern Plains. Custard Smith of the Low West. Katya Canopy newly of the Forest of Unspeakable Things. You are all charged with trespassing, spying, aiding known criminals, theft, destruction of property, grievous injury to gnomekind, and criminal intent. In addition, Harold Macinaw of the Eastern Plains, you are charged with treasonous acts."

He pauses, his voice echoing through the round room. "How do you all plead?"

"I think I speak on behalf of us all," Macinaw says, his voice strong and echoing, "when I say we plead not guilty, Your Eminence."

"Your pleas have been entered into the record," the gnome says. "First witness against the accused is called forth. Master Constantine Botch, Healer of the Peoples."

The Healer is dragged into the room from a different door than we came through. His arms and legs are shackled like ours, his head lolling around his shoulders like he might not be conscious. His fanny pack is missing. A goblin thrusts him, barely standing, in front of the dais where the two rows of gnomes sit.

"Master Botch, we have a few questions for you."

The iron door clangs shut.

The Healer looks so tiny in this giant room. His possum nose is droopy, his shoulders hunched, but he turns his head slightly and sees us. His little yam face brightens and he lifts one of his shackled hands to give us a wave.

These are some scary gnomes looking down on us. It's like their eyes are made of coal. I can't see a flicker of anything friendly up there.

"Master Constantine Botch, Healer of the Peoples," the

white-bearded gnome says. His voice sounds like a sports announcer, if announcing soon-to-be-dead people's names was a sport.

"I am he," the Healer replies, standing up straight.

"What know you of these yoomans?"

"They are my Buck and my Lizzie," the Healer says. He is speaking slowly, his voice calm and solid. "They the bravest of all the peoples."

"Master Botch, these are yoomans, not Flipside peoples," a woman says from the second row.

"They have Flipside hearts, they do," the Healer says. "Flipside hearts of the past. Of the better days. Bravest and strong. Kindly and selfless-like."

My heart swells for the little dude. I want to rush to the front of the room and steal him out of here. He has only been kind to us, and look where it's gotten him.

"Did you assist these yoomans as they trespassed and plundered through sacred lands?" the gnome with the long white beard asks.

"I joined a mission of rescuing," the Healer says, his head high. "I helped save a stolen gnome and a missing yooman. I did that."

"That violates the Law of the Land, Master Botch."

"I am not a gnome," the Healer says. "My laws are guided

by my head, and by this part right here." He points to his chest. "Little Healer heart just as big as any other heart."

I look at Lizzie. Her jaw is set and she's staring straight ahead. She wants to pop someone in the face. This is the same look she has in earth science when Mr. Hoffman says global warming is just a theory.

"Take him away," White Beard says. The goblins drag the Healer off, but not before he gives us another small wave. I wave back. "Yoomans," White Beard says. "What do you have to say for yourselves?"

Lizzie clenches her jaw and continues to stare angrily. I stand up. "Well, sir, uh, sirs. And ma'ams. Um. As a human, I have to say that my heart is one that just wants to help. I am a huge fan of Flipside." White Beard's eyes narrow and Lizzie's gaze swings to me. She clears her throat. "Wh-what I mean is," I stammer, "that I'm very honored to be here. I would never do anything to hurt your world or, uh, change anything here. I'm here to help, actually. Smith came Topside and—" Smith puts his face in his hands. "Well," I say, feeling sweat drip from my armpits down my arms, "what I mean to say is that there's this prophecy?"

Lizzie stands up and interrupts me. "What Buck is trying to say is that we love and respect gnomes and gnome-kind. Everything we do is out of love and respect." She pulls at my elbow to get me to sit. I'm not sure what she said is right, though. Do the gnomes care if we love them? I doubt it.

"We think you're super-powerful," I say, in a last-ditch effort. "I mean, not that we don't, uh, love you . . ." I throw a glance at Lizzie and can tell she's fuming that I won't stop talking. She's blinking at me in a continuous stream of angry eyelash swats. "But, like, as a hero. As a man, if you will." I puff out my chest and Smith and Katya both roll their eyes. "I understand that love doesn't really conquer all. Might is, uh, mighty. And we respect your might, and are here to add to that. We—"

White Beard holds up his hand. "We've heard enough. Gnomes? Anything you have to say?"

Smith stands. "You know my opinions regarding yoomans and prophecies. You know I am willing to do whatever it takes to maintain gnome power."

"We know you are reckless and dangerous," White Beard spits at him.

"But our end goals are the same," Macinaw says. "Surely you can understand that?"

"I can understand you are a treasonous old gnome, sharing secrets with Topside peoples who do not deserve such sacred knowledge. I understand you are headstrong and prone to believing fairy tales. While our ultimate goals may be similar, your means are dangerous and cannot be condoned."

Katya says nothing. She's trying to loosen her hands, which are shackled facing each other to prevent her from using her magic.

White Beard turns around and motions for the other gnomes to move closer. There is an echoing sound of wooden chairs scraping across stone as they all slide their seats back and stand up. They move to huddle around him. After a few minutes, the gnomes move back to their seats.

White Beard turns to face us. "It is evident that the charges raised against the five of you are true, and I don't wish to waste the time of my council by stretching out matters any further. What remains to be decided is punishment. Each charge can earn up to five hundred years in the dungeons for the yoomans. However, after discussion, we are inclined to make an example of you. These kinds of crimes are not to be tolerated and must be dealt with publicly and swiftly."

He slams a gavel onto a small lectern in front of him. "On behalf of the Gnome Syndicate, I sentence you all to death."

The fancy, scary gnomes all say, "Hear, hear."

My knees go a little weak and I hear Lizzie gasp. Macinaw is silent, his lips forming a thin line nearly lost in his beard. Smith stares straight ahead with no expression, and Katya's fingers twitch like they wish they could grab a handful of mindbombs and go crazy up in here.

"We shall commence immediately," White Beard says. "Jailers, to the pits we go."

"Pits?" I squeak out.

"Acid viper pits," White Beard answers with a chill in his voice. "An unfortunately quick death, if you ask me. But the gnomes love to watch."

I look at Lizzie and mouth the word *SNAKES*. I feel like I might barf. Lizzie looks back and her eyes are sparking. She looks aaaaaangry. I don't blame her. I'm angry, too. But mostly scared. Really, super, stuck-in-a-trash-compactor-with-a-giant-snake-worm-thing scared.

White Beard marches out of the room as goblins seize our arms and drag us after him.

19

One good thing about being sentenced to death by being thrown into a pit of acid vipers is that you have to wait for your audience to assemble, so you have some time to mull over everything that's gotten you to this point.

I guess maybe that's not such a good thing.

"Is this really happening?" I ask no one in particular.

Lizzie is so angry she's practically shooting steam from her ears. Smith and Katya look very stoic, with clamped lips and narrowed eyes. Macinaw is staring at me, which I find less reassuring than I would have thought a few days ago. There's an uptick to one side of his mouth, like a very subtle half smile. He seems to be kind of stoked that I'm about to get tossed into this pit. Doesn't he realize he's going in with me?

No one has said anything since we were dragged outside. We're standing on a high wooden platform, all tied together with a length of chain between our shackles. Any slight movement from one of us ripples through the others, so we all have to stand very still in order not to accidentally fling ourselves into the pit when someone tries to scratch their nose. The Healer is shackled to a post just behind us. I guess they'll throw him in for dessert.

The "pit" is actually a kind of concrete cistern thing with squares cut out at gnome eyeball height at the bottom. This way they have a good view of us being eaten or stung or melted or whatever by the vipers.

Our platform is situated just over the open top. I peer over the edge and see a writhing mass of putrid green and black. My stomach is writhing even more. There has to be something we can do. I tug at the shackle around my wrist, which makes the chain tug at Smith's wrist. He gives me laser eyes. If only. If I could shoot metal-melting lasers from my eyes all our problems would be solved. I would also be forbidden to ride the school bus, I bet. Win-win.

Gnomes are arriving by the wagonload and congregating around the bottom edge of the cistern. They are laughing and passing around things that look like cupcakes and generally acting like they're at a party. There are a few trolls down there, too. The gnomes are leading them by chain leashes and the trolls are laden with bags of food and other stuff. They're being treated like donkeys. This makes me think of donkeys and how *they're* treated. Man, why is everyone the worst?

Smith looks into the pit and Katya looks up at the sky. Lizzie has angry tears running down her face. Macinaw alternates between staring straight ahead and straight at me. I'm sure they're all thinking what I'm thinking. This is not what we had planned *at all*. Except maybe Macinaw is planning to eat me? I don't know what the deal is with that guy.

"A fine couple of days' work, if I do say so myself." It's Maori, walking over to us on the platform. He's just come up the metal ladder bolted to the side of the cistern. Katya spits at him, but he ignores her.

"Nasty business, these acid vipers," Maori says. "First they burn you, then they bite you, then they burn you some more, then they eat your paralyzed body." He pretends to shiver. "Lesson learned, I guess?" He smiles and the awful tattoos on his face bend and twist.

I'm starting to get really, really nervous. The crowd below is huge now, and the members of the Syndicate have all climbed onto the little stage built behind where we're standing on the wooden platform.

White Beard arrives, climbing stiffly off the ladder and standing on the wooden platform where we're all chained together. He gives us each an appraising look; then he walks up the couple of stairs to the stage where the other High Council gnomes sit. Once on the stage, he stands in front of a podium and bangs his gavel.

I feel a mixture of almost barfing and almost fainting, and I look at Lizzie and feel so, so sorry that I've gotten her into this. She looks at me, her face loose and frowning, and she shakes her head. I'd reach out for her hand, so that we could go into the pit holding on to each other, but the chains won't let me. There's just enough give for me to stuff my hands in my pocket instead. I squeeze Jan's rock.

OMG. Duh! Duh! DUUUUH! I'm such a dope! I'm a rockmouth! Why have I been moping this whole time instead of doing something? I lift the rock as close to my mouth as I can and whisper, "Find help. Please don't let them throw us in the pit of acid vipers."

A loud murmur fills the area. At first I think it's the crowd getting restless, but no. The murmur is in my head. It's like a million different voices all talking at once, faster and faster until it's a really loud buzz.

Lizzie is looking at me and her mouth is moving. I can't hear what she's saying, but her eyebrows are low like she's worried. I jerk my hands up, wishing I could grab my ears, and both Lizzie and Smith are propelled closer to the edge of the pit. I can't help it, though. The noise is so loud, my head is going to split in half.

The buzz dies down just enough for me to hear Lizzie yell, "Buck! Careful!" Then White Beard clears his throat and says, "Gentle gnomes, we have gathered you this grim afternoon to witness the—" but he never gets a chance to finish.

A bajillion rocks come rolling into the square. Instantly, there is chaos. And fire. How is there fire? Rocks are tumbling everywhere, rolling down hills, massing together to make giant writhing rocks made of smaller rocks, chasing gnomes, crashing so hard into the cistern we are all being jostled uncomfortably close to the edge.

I look over my shoulder, and from my high vantage point I can see gnomes fleeing for their wagons, some even forgoing the wagons and just running straight through the prairie grasses as rocks chase them. The High Council gnomes seem terribly confused up on their stage, even as they topple off and run around with fire streaming from their beards. *Where* is the fire coming from?

I don't know how this is happening, but the cistern around my feet is coming apart. I guess it's not really made of concrete, but made of a bunch of stones all set together? Rocks are flying over my feet and smashing into the chains around my ankles. I see the same thing happening to everyone else, too. The only problem is that it's messing with our balance. YOU try holding still while the cistern under your feet falls apart and is simultaneously beating at your feet. We're all wobbling like crazy, and I'm worried the enthusiastic rocks are accidentally going to cause us to fall into the viper pit. But they make fast work of the feet shackles.

"Lean over!" I yell. "We have to all do it at once so they can get to our chains and we won't fall. On three!" Smith, Katya, Macinaw, and Lizzie are all looking at me as I carefully mime how we'll all bend down at the same time. "One! Two! Three!" We all kneel. It's a little herky-jerky, but no one falls, thank goodness. The rocks go to town, beating and smashing at the chains between our hands and the ones linking us all together.

White Beard's face is slick and red, his eyes bulging as he watches the chaos. He struggles for a moment and then spits out, "Apprehend these criminals!" There's a scramble and someone yells, "Which criminals? You mean the rocks?" Everyone but White Beard is completely ignoring us, trying to save their own tiny skins.

Not that I can blame them. The rocks are small, but they're coming in huge bunches, that's for sure, and they are not shy about flinging themselves at gnome heads.

I see two rocks crack into each other, creating a spark. The spark catches a beard on fire. Aha. That makes sense, but ouch. I feel a little bad for the gnomes. But only a little.

Smith is waving his arms at me, broken chains dangling. I look over my shoulder to see what he's pointing at. As the little rocks disappear in groups, chasing gnomes here and there, a massive rock has appeared on the horizon. It's not just one rock, though. I take off my glasses and clean them on my shirt. When I put them back on I see that the giant rock is rolling along on a wave of smaller rocks. There's a rider, *made* of rocks (what!), using one hand to hold on to thick rope reins on the giant rock. With the other hand it's holding a huge flag. The flag has an embroidered picture of the Troll Queen's crest.

The gigantic boulder rolls up to the cistern and the rider uses its reins-holding rock hand to motion for us all to climb on. The Troll Queen flag whips past my face as I scramble onto the rock. The Healer gets on behind me. Hob's pants! I almost forgot about the tiny guy! Thankfully, the rocks didn't.

The rock person/thing driving this huge boulder throws the Troll Queen flag at White Beard and it lands on the platform in front of him, stabbing into the wood with a twang. White Beard's red, howling face shrinks as we roll away. I am terrified and relieved and confused and afraid and pretty much every descriptive word all at once.

I mean, really. To be very honest, riding a giant, speeding boulder without immediately falling off is not one of the easiest things a person (or gnome or Healer) can do. However, it definitely beats being burned and stung and then eaten alive by acid vipers. At least for now.

The boulder is really fast, and in no time we're far enough away from Hob City (that was Hob City! OMG!) that we can't even see the cistern on the horizon. As we roll away, though, I have a sickening thought.

"Wait! Wait! Stop!" I shout. "The mace! It's back at Hob City! DANG."

The rock wave under us slows down until we stop. "We have to go back," I say. "It's pointless to go anywhere without the mace."

"Agreed," Macinaw and Smith say together.

"Do we really need the mace, Buck?" Lizzie asks. "It didn't work with those trolls in the desert, remember? Don't you think it's time to forget all this prophecy nonhome?"

"Nonsense?" I say. "I mean, yeah, I hate to admit that I've grown to really believe the prophecy, but I do. I feel like I'm here to do something important. Don't you? Sure, I feel like maybe I'd rather be at home, curled up in my comfy bed, eating a grilled cheese sandwich and rereading *Gnome-a-geddon*, but also? We're on an adventure, Lizzie. I actually feel important. I've never felt important before."

Lizzie sighs. "I'm not saying you're not important, Buck, I'm just saying we almost got killed back there. Like really really for real almost killed. I'm feeling pretty done with almost getting killed. Let's find Willy and go home."

"We need the mace," I argue. "I don't see how we'll be able to win her freedom without the Troll Vanquishing Mace. We will get *actually* killed if we don't have it to protect us."

"The boy makes an excellent point," Macinaw says. "Having the correct weaponry when entering a fight is imperative to one's success."

Smith nods gravely. Katya rolls her eyes.

"You want to find this little girl as badly as Buck does?" Katya asks Lizzie.

I think it's the first time she's said my name and not called me a troll.

"Yes!" Lizzie answers. "And I don't want to waste any more time."

"Okay, then," Katya says, nodding once. "We will go find her."

"No!" I say, feeling my heartbeat quicken. "I just explained. And he did, too!" I point at Macinaw. "We need the mace to save Willy. We—"

"We will go without you," Katya says simply. "You go find your mace, chase your silly prophecy, and Lizzie and I will go find your sister and return her home."

"What?" I say, feeling more and more frustrated. "That's not how it works. *I* have to save her. *I* need the mace. You can't just go off by yourselves. You need the mace to save her! Plus . . . this is *my* quest."

"I'm going with Katya," Lizzie says. She jumps off the rock and dusts off her pants.

"Wait. What?" I shout down at her. "No! You're *what*?"

"I'm going with Katya," Lizzie says. Katya jumps down after her and they both look up at me and Smith and Macinaw. The Healer is chewing his claw nervously.

"I don't . . . I don't understand," I say. "Why in the world would you go with *her*? We're in this together. We have been since the beginning. Since *before* the begin-ning, really. You're my . . . you're *mine*." I can't decide if I want to jump down after her, or stay on top of the boulder shouting. Shouting feels like it gives me more power.

"Can you even hear yourself, Buck? I'm *yours*?" Lizzie looks at me in disgust. She's never looked at me like that before.

"No," I say, feeling flustered. "That's not really what I meant. I just mean, we're a team, you know? We came here together, and—"

"I can't make you understand this, Buck. I can't make you understand how this whole time you've been trying to save me, or keep me out of harm's way. You've insisted on doing things on your own when it's more dangerous that way. You don't think of me as equal. You don't think this story is also my story. Not even close. If you have to ask why I would want to go with Katya, why I would think the prophecy is silly, well . . . then your answer is somewhere in those feelings."

"Huh?" I can't make sense of any of this. "Is this because of the mindbomb? Are you feeling crazy because of that? Healer! Is Lizzie having some kind of relapse or something?" I'm genuinely worried about her. She sounds like some conspiracy theorist or something.

"Oh, Buck." Lizzie's look of disgust has changed to disappointment. "When you can figure out that *every* story doesn't need a boy to save a girl, let me know. And when you realize that the smart girl is good for something other than comic relief, then you can come *find* me." She and Katya have started walking away.

"*How* can I let you know? *How* can I find you? I won't know where you are!" I feel panic crawling up my spine. "I know how important you are, Lizzie. You're like . . . like my flashlight, showing me where to go, keeping me from being too scared!" What am I going to do without Lizzie? She can't leave me. Not here. Not now. Not ever!

"You're the one who has it all figured out, Buck. You're the one who's going to save the day. I'm only getting in your way, remember? I'm just another girl who needs to be protected and saved. You have a whole big prophecy to fulfill. It should be WAY easier now without me hanging around."

"No, Lizzie! You're twisting my words. That's not what I meant at all."

"We should move faster." Katya raises her hands and the wind picks up.

Lizzie looks back at me and her face is stone. But not the kind of stone I can speak to or understand. "But what happens when I find Willy? How will you get home?" I shout at her.

"You don't think I'll find her first?" She laughs an angry chuckle. "You don't think I'll find her at all, do you? You don't think I can figure out a way home on my own? You think I need a boy helping me every step of the way?"

"That's not what I said, Lizzie!"

She whips around and I can tell she's *really* mad now. Her eyes are flashing, her hands clenched into fists. "I am sick of this place. I'm trying really hard not to be sick of you, Buck, I'm really trying. But you need to *think*. You need to get a grip on what is real and what isn't. And what Macinaw is actually like versus what he's like in your head." She gives Macinaw a sour look and then transfers it to me. "I'm going with Katya to find Willy and you can't stop me."

Katya gives them a boost of wind and they shoot forward a few yards. "Willy and I will *see* you at home!" Lizzie yells over her shoulder. I'm not sure how to answer her. She's really leaving? Right now? We're at the penultimate part of the story. This isn't when the crew is supposed to break up.

The Healer gives me a helpless look and then scrambles down the boulder. "I have to go with this girl," he says.

"Both those girls. Gotta make sure they stay healthy. You know." He's running after them and I shout, "They don't want you to save them, Healer! And . . . and . . . what about me? I need to stay healthy, too!" But he's already out of earshot.

"Women." Macinaw shakes his head. "So entitled. So defiant. Am I right?" Smith nods and I feel really uncomfortable.

"Are we going to get the mace, or are you going to go cry after your girlfriend?" Smith asks.

"She's not my girlfriend," I say, feeling an embarrassing lump growing in my throat. She's more than that. She's my *best* friend. My only friend. And she just walked away. I take a deep breath and square my shoulders.

Well, fine. It's a race, then. We'll see who finds Willy first.

"Let's go," I say to the rock driver. "We need to get back to Hob City and find the Troll Vanquishing Mace." The little rocks start spinning under the big rock and propel us back the way we came, this time a little bit faster because we're two people and one Healer lighter.

As we move toward Hob City, it occurs to me that the driver of this boulder was holding a Troll Queen flag when he appeared to save the day. What the heck was that all about?

I'm about to ask him when he stops the rock and motions for us to get down. Before I can say anything, I hear a voice in my head, "You must go alone from here. We will await your orders."

He's right. You can't really sneak into a city when you're riding a gigantic boulder. For one thing, the boulder is super-loud. That seems strange, I know, but all those little rocks underneath it are grinding and popping and they make a racket. Also, an eight-foot boulder isn't exactly camouflaged in a meadow of green grass.

This is why Smith and Macinaw and I start army-crawling through the tall grass that surrounds Hob City. We need to sneak into the city unseen. I'll have to ask the boulder about that Troll Queen flag when we get back.

We come over a rise, and I see the cistern in the not-too-far distance. The top is crumbled, but the rest seems intact. The wooden platforms that encircled the opening of the pit have all crumbled to the ground. There are a few gnomes wandering around assessing the damage, but there's no sign of White Beard or any of the High Council members. No sign of Maori, either. And, of course, no sign of the mace.

Yeah, this should be really easy. Sigh.

Having only seen the dungeons and the courtroom of the High Council building, it's hard to gauge how big the city is. Like most everything built by the gnomes, it's almost completely underground. But I can see pyramids of glass dotting the ground all around the cistern. Skylights, just like in the courtroom. Perfect!

"Come on," I whisper to Smith and Macinaw, and motion for them to follow me. I army-crawl as fast as I can to the first skylight and peer in. It's hard to see through the wavy glass, but it looks like a room full of desks below. No mace. We move to the next one. A bunch of busy gnomes stand over stovetops, stirring big bowls. This reminds me how hungry I am. Maybe if we find the mace fast we can also sneak into the kitchen to get a snack. Very likely, I'm sure.

We go on like this for what feels like hours, peering into skylights, seeing nothing of importance, and moving to the next one. The sun is low in the sky now. Hunger and exhaustion are making my hands a little shaky.

Smith and Macinaw are way off in the distance, each checking out the skylights that are closest to them. This building is HUGE. Or, I guess it's a building? Maybe these skylights are for the whole city? Man, we're going to be here forever.

I'm peeking down into the pyramid-shaped skylight at my feet. It's dark in the room, but I can make out a bunch of bookshelves down below. There are a few pedestals with things on top. Statues, maybe. There are a comfy-looking couch, a desk in a corner, and what's that on the desk? I smush my glasses as close to my eyes as possible and peer down. Is that the mace on the desk? My heart pounds. I think it is! I stand up briefly and wave my arms, trying to get Smith and Macinaw's attention. They come running as soon as they see me. A few minutes later, they're huffing and puffing as we all look through the skylight.

"We'll have to move fast," I say. "Grab it and go. This looks like an important office."

Smith nods. "It definitely belongs to someone in the High Council."

"In and out," I say, pretending like I'm floating in the air, with my arms and legs suspended. "Like Tom Cruise in *Mission: Impossible*. Anyone have any rope?" Suddenly, the way we're going to get the mace seems like something we should have discussed earlier. Like maybe when we were on the speeding rock heading back here.

Macinaw and Smith look at me like I just asked if anyone can sprout wings. Then Smith hauls off and kicks the skylight, cracking the glass. "We. Are. Getting. This. Mace. Today." He grunts, saying each word with a kick. "We. Have. Come. This. Far. We. Are. Not. Leaving. Withou—" The glass shatters noisily, tinkling down into the office.

"Dude!" I yell. "I thought we were going to talk about a stealthy way to get in and out. Not smash and grab."

"Smash and grab sounds fine with me," Macinaw says, and leaps through the skylight. It has to be at least a ten-foot drop. The guy might be kind of a jerk, but he's pretty fearless. Smith leaps in after him. I figure this will probably hurt less than falling through the trees with Jan, so I jump, too.

Luckily, I land right on top of Macinaw, so my body is nicely cushioned when I crash to the ground. We push apart and both run straight for the mace. Smith is busy shoving the desk chair under the knobs of the round double doors that seem to be the only entrance and exit to the room, not counting the bashed-in skylight.

"Smart!" I yell over my shoulder to Smith. We've made enough noise that surely every gnome and goblin and troll in the building is heading our way.

"Get the mace!" he yells back. Macinaw is actually closer to the mace than I am, but he's just standing there staring at it, his mouth open slightly. I reach out to grab it just as he reaches out, but I manage to get it first. He pulls his hand back quickly and smiles at me. He swallows hard and takes a step away from me, glancing at Smith. Smith moves away from the chair under the doors and comes toward us.

Relief washes over me as I hold the mace. This detour feels like it took way too much time. I might be weak with hunger and lack of sleep, but I'm ready to find Willy and get her back. I'm ready to get home and kick Fake Buck to the curb. I don't even care why he's there anymore. I just want my bed and my mom and a grilled cheese sandwich. Nobody ever talks about how hungry everyone must be in

Narnia or wandering through the Ministry of Magic, but man, I'm starving. I think I've been starving *ever* since I got here. Probably, writers think this is boring stuff that kids don't really care about when they're reading about these great adventures, but as someone who is on a supposedly great adventure right now, can I just say, I don't smell very good, and I'm so hungry I am like a cartoon character who sees meat when he looks at anything. This mace looks like a chicken leg right now. Serious.

"Ready?" Macinaw asks.

"Hmm?" I say. I didn't realize he was talking to me.

"Ready," Smith says.

And then, weirdly, they're both on top of me. Hurting me.

"Ow! OW! You guys! What the heck?!"

"Get his arms!" Smith yells.

"I'm not accidentally touching that thing while *he's* touching it," Macinaw yells back. "*You* get his arms."

"You guys!" I holler. "Ouch! Let go!" Macinaw is digging his fingernails into my wrist. I try to shake him off, but he's holding on tight.

"Drop the mace, son," Macinaw says. "Drop it now and this can all be over."

"What are you *talking* about?" I pant, writhing around, trying to get out from under the grappling gnomes. "I have it for *us*, you weirdo!" I'm on my back, trying to kick them off while still holding the mace, when I see a shadow pass over the broken skylight. The shadow gets darker and darker until it becomes an enormous scaly head with enormous pointy teeth. And then next to the scaly head I see a very familiar mop of brown hair. Am I dead? Hallucinating?

"Buck!" shouts the familiar head.

"Willy?!" I shout back.

"Hang on!" she yells. The scaly head pushes its way through the skylight, its neck as long as a boa constrictor. Willy slides down the neck and lands on her feet not far away from our ruckus. Macinaw and Smith have slowed their pummeling enough for me to scramble up and away from them. I run to Willy. There's no time for hugs or greetings, though, because Macinaw and Smith are back on me, trying to wrestle me to the ground. The dragon seems agitated at all the movement and noise, and I am agitated that *everyone* has gone insane.

"You guys, what is your *deal*?!" I shout. I wriggle away from them, spinning and contorting away from their hands. Years of wrestling with Willy are now serving me well.

The dragon snorts smoke into the room, making us all cough.

"Give it to me!" Willy yells at me. She pats the dragon's snout and whispers something to it. It pulls its head up and out of the skylight.

"What?" I yell back.

"GIVE IT TO ME!" she hollers.

"No, Willy, I mean *what*? Give you what?"

"The mace, dummy!" she shouts. "Throw it over here!"

Without even questioning her, I do it, and instantly Smith and Macinaw are off me and heading toward her.

"Oh, great idea, Willy," I say, charging after them. But Willy swings the mace, and it grazes Smith's face. He lets out a yowl you can probably hear Topside. The scratch on his face sizzles and bubbles like it's been splashed with acid. Smith stumbles back, his hands grappling at the wound.

"What the?" I look at Willy, who is staring in wonder at the mace. She swings it at Smith again, and when it connects with his arm, he flies back at least ten feet and way up into the air. His back smashes against a bookshelf and he falls to the ground with a grunt. Macinaw has backed very far away and is watching with his mouth hanging open like a dog badly in need of a drink of water.

"Willy!" I shout. "What are you doing?!"

The mace isn't supposed to inflict any kind of damage on gnomes. It's a *Troll* Vanquishing Mace. Plus, I am the cho-

254

sen one. I am the Halfling. I am the hero of this story. I—

Smith is raging mad now. He gets to his feet and charges Willy. She casually holds the mace out in front of her like a flashlight, and when Smith is about five feet away she flicks the mace a couple of inches up, like she's shaking off a fly.

Smith cries out, as even the tiniest flick of the mace sends a scorching line of heat across his arm. His arm and his face look like someone has held them to a campfire. All it takes is a tiny tap of the mace on the top of his head and he crumples into a ball, unconscious.

Willy looks at the mace and then at Smith. She looks at me and at Macinaw. "Wow," she says. Then, "Is that Macinaw?"

I nod.

She casually swings the mace in his direction and he takes about five giant steps back. I kneel over Smith, remembering something. I stick my hand in his pockets and find what I've remembered. It's the tiny, crumbling scroll that fell out of the hilt when we first found the mace.

Willy comes over, and she leans in so close I can smell her sweat and just the littlest trace of her shampoo. Lavender. I have to stop for a moment and give her a bone-crushing hug. "Willy," I whisper. "I'm so glad you're okay."

She smiles. "What do you have there?" I carefully unfurl the scroll all the way. I kneel on the floor next to the still-unconscious Smith, holding the scroll flat at the corners with my palms.

"Willy." My voice is small. I clear my throat. "Willy, look." She kneels down next to me.

"What?"

I point and she leans even lower, so she can make out the fading script.

It doesn't make any sense. There's no way—

Only he who is part of troll and part of newer kind can be the master of the mace.

"Shouldn't that say *part of gnome*?" Willy asks. "Shouldn't gnomes be using the Troll Vanquishing Mace to vanquish trolls?"

"He who is part of troll?" What? "This is a *Gnome* Vanquishing Mace?" I look at Smith, see his smoking face and burning arm. I look at Macinaw breathing heavily, his back up against a wall. I look back down at the scroll. I look back up. "And only a *troll* Halfling can wield it?" My brain is zipping around in about eight different directions. It can't land on any idea just yet, there are so many crazy things flinging around between my ears. It's like a movie where I hear people's voices echoing in my head from memories.

Lizzie saying something about Smith saying I'm a Halfling. Me saying something about my dad being nearly seven feet tall. Jan calling me brother.

"I'M HALF-TROLL?!" I shout it way louder than I mean to. I motion to Willy and then to myself. "*WE'RE* HALF-TROLL??" I feel like my head is floating about three feet above my body. I look at Macinaw. "So why . . . why do you guys want the mace, then? You want to vanquish *gnomes?* Are you trying to take over the High Council or something?" I'm pacing now, trying to work everything out. I point to Smith. "Do you think he knew I was half-troll all along?" Smith is waking up and I drop to my knees next to him. "Did you know? DID YOU? Did you know Willy and I are half-troll?!" One look at his face tells me he did.

"So, but, I . . ." I sit on the floor and look up at Willy. "I don't. I don't understand."

"What's going on in here?" Two gnomes come bursting through the double doors at the other side of the room. The chair flies across the floor as if it was made of Tinker-toys. There are two giant trolls next to them. Their arms and legs are chained, but the chains are long enough for them to move pretty easily. Their blue faces are scrunched in anger until they see the mace in Willy's hand. It's like they've seen the sun for the first time. Or tasted ice cream for the first time. Or reached the final level on the Triumphant Gnome Syndicate game and defeated the Troll Queen, except, maybe not that exactly. They still stand by the gnomes' sides, but they are looking intently at Willy.

"You again!" one of the gnomes shouts, looking straight at me. I think he must have been part of the group of gnomes behind White Beard. "Seize him!" he shouts, motioning for the trolls to get me.

Willy flicks the mace at the talking gnome and he crashes back into the hallway outside the open doors. The trolls whip their heads over their shoulders to watch him fly through the air. The other gnome doesn't say anything, he just bolts from the room like there's a sale on courage in the next room over. Smith groans and lays his blistered head back on the floor.

"Listen to your master!" Macinaw spits at the trolls. "Get that mace."

"You are not our master," one of the trolls says. He smiles at Willy. She smiles back.

"I didn't mean me, you imbecile!" Macinaw shouts. His face is turning bright red. "I meant the poor soul blasted into the hallway. He said to seize the mace, and you better seize it."

"Actually," the other troll says, smiling broadly, "I think he said to seize the boy. Did he say that, Gerald?" The first troll nods. "But I don't think we will seize the boy, will we, Gerald?" Gerald shakes his head. "I think we will help the boy and the Halfling escape. That's what I think we're going to do." Gerald nods again. Both trolls have giddy expressions on their faces as they move closer to us. They wince as the chains rub up against their wrists and ankles, sizzling and smoking, but even as they wince they grin.

"You'll do no such thing, you hammers!" Macinaw yells. "You doorknobs!" Little bits of spit are gathering at the corners of his mouth. He looks like a crazy animal. "You'll help me and the Sheriff of Flipside to safety, and you will turn these children over to the proper authorities."

"I don't think we will," Gerald says. He's looking down at Smith with a mixture of anger and pity, his smile faltering. "I think the authorities have not been proper for a while now."

Macinaw frantically looks at Smith, who is in no condition to move on his own. He looks at me and his face contorts into a gargoyle-ish mask. "You cannot stay alive."

"Um, what?" I say, taking a large step closer to the closest troll, who seems way friendlier than Macinaw at this point.

"Smith brought you down here to find me, is that what he told you?" Macinaw lunges at me and I jump back. Willy flicks the mace and he howls as a red streak appears across his arm. "We engineered my little poof, so that he could get you here. He'd been watching you, did you know that? The boy whose father is so tall. And how convenient that you were a fan of the books. It made things so much easier. Get you here, have you find the mace, let you think you're fulfilling the prophecy, then destroy the mace, kill you, kill the prophecy, and ensure gnome rule forevermore." His eyes glaze over a bit as he rubs the injury on his arm. He quietly recites the prophecy: "*The world is cracked open. With a mighty swing from unpracticed arms, the secret-knowing Halfling wields the mace. The Halfling restores balance as the bruising fates bring about a new day, and what's lost is found again, the world forever changed.*" His eyes focus and he looks at me, hard. "We don't want balance restored. We want gnome rule forevermore."

"You're monologuing," I say. "Haven't you ever read a book or seen a movie? The villain always monologues just before he gets killed. You better watch out."

Macinaw laughs at me like I'm the funniest joke ever. Everything he says sits in my stomach like a stone. Is it true, I wonder? Smith was just going to kill me after I found the mace for him? I do not like learning I've been a stupid pawn, just wandering around in some long con, waiting to be killed. Stupid red shirt! I want to rip it off my chest, but you can't actually do things like that in real life.

Macinaw's eyes are wide. I can see the whites all the way around them. He's pacing the room, giving a wide berth to the trolls and Willy. "We had it all planned. And things got a little bumpy for a while there, with the High Council interfering. Their insistence on ignoring the prophecy will be their downfall." He lunges for the mace again, when he thinks Willy isn't looking. She casually points it at him and he cries out, grabbing his leg.

I look at Willy. "Dad's a troll?" My mind feels buzzy.

She shrugs. "He *is* super-tall."

"But he's not *blue!*"

Macinaw is right next to me now, and Willy tosses the mace to me quickly. I swing it, but when it connects with Macinaw's arm it does nothing except make him look down in surprise. There's no red streak, no sizzling, no bleeding, nothing. A surprised grin snakes across his face and he dives at me. I throw the mace back at Willy and she catches it like it's magnetized and her palms are iron.

Macinaw yowls in frustration and turns to the trolls again. "Get that mace, you mudbrains. Now. Do you want to see gnome rule end? You'll lose everything you have. Warm beds, good food, work to do. Your lives will become meaningless without masters to serve. You'll have no impetus to do anything except laze around. You'll grow fat. You'll starve to death."

Can he even hear himself? None of what he says makes any sense.

"I do not think we shall grow fat or starve to death," Gerald says. "I think we shall enjoy a freedom we have not enjoyed for decades."

Macinaw lets out a frustrated scream and he charges Willy. She's ready for him, though, and whacks him across the neck with the mace. He's bleeding now. A lot. He's trying to talk, but only burbles come out of his mouth. Gerald runs to him and tries to apply pressure to the wound, but Macinaw spits at him and wriggles away.

Gerald looks at Willy and then at me. What can we do? Macinaw grapples at the wound on his neck and again Gerald approaches him, having torn a bit of his pant leg off to use as a bandage.

"No!" Macinaw gurgles as blood seeps through his fingers. "Get your dirty hands away from me." Gerald takes a step back. Macinaw's face is almost as white as his beard now. There's a growing pool of blood.

Willy moves closer to me. Her eyes are wide; her mouth opens but no words come out. I snatch the bit of pant leg from Gerald and run to press it against Macinaw's wound.

Macinaw is kicking out, grasping his neck, but then suddenly his body stops moving. His head lolls to the side, though his eyes are still open. I pull my bloody hands back. I think he's dead.

"We should go," the troll who is not Gerald says. "The others will come looking."

Smith is in and out of consciousness, still on the floor. I kneel down next to him, not knowing what to feel. My hands are sticky with Macinaw's blood. "You were going to kill me?" He doesn't answer. I shake his shoulder and his eyes flutter open. "You were going to *kill* me?!"

"I couldn't . . ." He coughs. And for a moment I feel relief. But then he continues. "I couldn't let the prophecy come true." He coughs again, his eyes shutting. "I'm sorry, Buck, but it's the truth. I'd been visiting Topside for years, trying to pinpoint suspected trolls or those with troll blood. Your father is over six feet seven. Short for a troll, but tall for a yooman. I had to see. And then everything seemed to be true. You seemed to be the one. You were the boy to be destroyed."

For maybe the first time in my life, I'm speechless. I

don't know how to respond, so I don't. I just say "Bye, Smith. And good luck, I guess. With the High Council and the vipers and everything."

Gerald reaches for Willy's hand, lifts her to his shoulders, and then pushes her out of the broken skylight. Before I can say anything else, I'm lifted and pushed out of the skylight as well.

With their chains clanking, the two trolls push the desk under the skylight and then pull themselves up and out into the evening. Willy whistles hard and loud—I've never heard a noise like that come out of her before. The huge dragon appears and circles overhead.

I can't believe Willy just saw Macinaw die like that. I can't believe she *killed* him. She's going to have nightmares for the rest of her life. *I'm* going to have nightmares for the rest of my life. I glance at her, but she's standing there with her mouth in a tight line. She's not chewing her fingernails or worrying her Silly Putty. Her arms are loose at her side, her hand holding the mace's grip lightly, its spikes resting on the ground next to her feet. Her hair blows gently in the wind as she turns slowly to catch my eye. A single ray of sun breaks through the early-evening clouds and shines down on her. She looks lit from within; the dirt smeared on her face is like war paint. And in this moment it's like I can hear angels singing. The truth fills me like a deep breath, and understanding strikes hard. It's so obvious why the mace didn't work for me when I tried to use it. Willy is the answer to the prophecy, not me. Willy is the Halfling. Willy is the Chosen One.

21

If you've ever read a book or watched a movie where someone rides a dragon (a real dragon, a big one, not a tiny schnauzer-sized dragon), I will say right now, however they describe it can in no way actually capture how awesome it is. And I mean awesome in every sense of the word. Feeling those heavy, muscly wings beat under you, feeling the warmth of the scales as you hold on for dear life . . . it's terrifying and exhilarating, and something I will never forget, ever.

The wind whips so hard and fast we couldn't hear each other if we tried to talk, so I just stare at the Flipside countryside as we zoom over it. It's amazing how quickly the terrain changes. It doesn't make sense in human terms.

There are forests and deserts sprinkled everywhere. How can the ecosystem change like that? I guess maybe they're microenvironments just like the gnomes are micropeople? I have no idea, but it looks really cool from so high up.

Off in the distance, there are dark, rolling clouds on the horizon, and I give Willy a look. It's great being on this dragon, but heading into a storm doesn't seem very smart. She points at the clouds and nods. That's when I figure it out. Those aren't clouds at all. They're dark, rolling *mountains*.

Troll Mountain.

It's real.

It doesn't take long for the dragon's huge wings to propel us into the mountain range. The mountains aren't giant spiky things like you would think. This is no Mordor. They are gentle hills, really, green and almost blue—a kind of turquoise that comes from the shining needles of the trees. It's beautiful, really. And it smells like Christmas trees.

The dragon glides to a landing on top of a hill, and Willy takes my hand, helping me down. For the first time I realize she isn't still in her pajamas like I am. Her clothes are similar to Katya's. Billowy, comfy-looking pants, suspenders in an X shape across her chest, a button-up shirt like something Robin Hood would wear. With the mace slung over her shoulder, she looks like she belongs here. She is definitely not the worried and scared little sister I thought I was trying to save. In fact . . .

"You just saved me," I say, following her to a cave opening in the hill. "I've spent all this time trying to find you and save you and you just saved *me*."

Willy looks over her shoulder and smiles. "Yep."

We walk into the cave and after a few yards I can tell it's not like a cave at all. The walls are rough, but not dirty. The ground is smooth and clean. After a little way, we reach a metal door with a little speaker in the wall next to it. Willy jumps and smacks a button. "It's me!" she yells up at the speaker. "I got him." The door buzzes open and Willy swings it wide, marching down the hallway. I feel like we're in a castle, or at least what I would imagine a castle to be like. The walls are still rough, but there are fancy rugs under our feet. Rugs that show battles, a lot like the battles carved into the floors of the Academy, but on the rugs the trolls are the heroes.

There are doors peppered along the hallway. They aren't numbered or marked in any way, but Willy knows exactly where she's going. She pushes open one of the doors and I follow her. The room is cozy, with paintings on the walls, a big squishy couch, even a kitchen off to the side. I guess it's an apartment.

"You can sit down if you want," Willy says. "Do you want a drink of water or something?"

Suddenly I remember just how starving I am. "Water," I manage to sputter. "And a snack?" Willy's forehead is creased in concern. She looks a lot like Mom, actually. She goes into the kitchen while I sit on the couch. It feels like clouds, or a pile of cotton, or maybe sinking into the soft wool of a very big sheep. I could fall asleep for days.

Willy is back in two minutes with a cup of water and a plate of . . . something. "This isn't going to make my hair fall out or kill my pancreas, is it?" I ask, mouth watering even though I have no idea what it is.

"What?" Willy wrinkles her nose. "It's peaberry jam and crackers. Not much, but the fastest thing I could think of."

Peaberry. I wrack my brain to remember why I know that word. I shove a sticky cracker in my mouth and the taste comes back to me immediately. The peaberry tea! At the Healer's house. Sweet, with a hint of hot dogs.

"This is made with troll sweat?" I ask, spraying crackers as I chew like the starving person I am.

Willy laughs. "Yes. But just a little bit."

"You're here!" A very, very tall blue woman appears

from a narrow hallway at the other end of the room we're in. She's wearing an outfit similar to Willy's, and she has a small crown on her shining black hair. It is not made of bones. It's made of sparkling black stone. Obsidian, I bet. The troll woman holds her hand out to me, and I'm not sure what she wants. When I don't do anything or say anything, except dumbly crunch my crackers and peaberry jam, she just leans into me and gives me a tight hug. "You're safe now," she says in my ear. She smells like flowers . . . and hot dogs.

I don't know if you've ever been starving, like actually starving. If you have, you know that when you finally get food it tastes like the best thing you've ever eaten. You can't think of anything else, only the food in your mouth, only the way your empty stomach seizes as it finally has food to digest. You have this feeling of frantic eating-ness, and of extreme happiness, and also like you might puke at any second. So it's hard for me to actually understand the words the troll woman is saying. I'm safe? In a troll's apartment? Is that even where I am? Honestly, I don't care. I just want to sit on this squishy couch and eat these crackers for the next ten hundred years.

The troll woman releases me from her hug and smiles

down at me. "Your friends have told me so much about you. So has Willy."

Katya and Lizzie come down the hallway, both looking a little apprehensive. They're cleaned up, and Lizzie doesn't have the dark circles under her eyes anymore. Katya wears a shirt that isn't ripped. The Healer bobs around their legs, waving at me.

I stand up, surprised—more than surprised—to see them. Lizzie rushes to me and hugs me. "I'm sorry," she says. "I'm so sorry I just left you there."

Katya looks me up and down. "He looks okay to me," she says. "Not that I'm *not* happy to see you, troll. I just don't feel the need to gush." She nods at me and I nod back. The Healer leaps onto the couch and steals one of my crackers. I feel a quick instinct to push him off the couch and pull the cracker from his mouth, but I don't. I even suppress the growl I feel in my throat. He crunches the cracker and hugs me tight. "Buck, Buck, my Bucky Buck, you are just fine. You are here!" He releases me and claps his hands.

I've finally had enough to eat that my brain is starting to work again. "Someone," I say, "is going to have to tell me what's going on."

"We're about to take over Flipside," Willy says breathlessly. "It's gonna be huge. The trolls will finally be released from so many years of gnome rule. Buck, the world is about to change."

Who IS this girl in front of me?

"The mace was key," the troll woman says. "We can't thank you enough for finding it."

"Buck!" Willy says, leaning over to grab both of my shoulders with her hands. "You have to see what we're going to do with the mace. The trolls have been working on it for years and years. They've been waiting for just this moment. They knew someone had to fulfill the prophecy, and they knew that someone would be the one who has to wield the weapon. They've been going city by city, swapping changelings for the kids, so that the kids could be brought down here and tested. They've had zero hits until now. No Halflings, no hidden trolls, nothing. Until us. Well, until me." Her cheeks flush.

I have so many questions I'm not sure which one to ask first.

"I know you have a lot of questions," the troll woman says, holding up her hand as my mouth opens. "We'll answer them all. But first I want to show you something. Follow me?" She turns to go back down the narrow hallway. The Healer jogs alongside her huge strides, with Katya behind them.

"With this mace finally all the critters of Flipside will be liberated. Finally the rule of the gnomes will be over." He glances at Katya and then casts his gaze lower. "No offense meant."

"Oh, no offense, taken, Healer," Katya says. Her face is stern but her eyes are bright. "I am not proud of what gnomes have been doing for so long. Why do you think I went to live in the woods? I just . . . I couldn't be part of it, but I didn't want to take a dive into a pit of acid vipers, either." She shrugs, her lips bent into a guilty frown.

Lizzie and Willy reach out their hands to pull me up off the couch. After sitting and relaxing, all my muscles are screaming, "NO WAY, DO NOT MOVE AGAIN. IT IS TIME FOR SLEEPING." My bones ache, my head is swimming.

"Just take a look at this," Willy says, holding my elbow and helping me walk down the hallway. "Then you can rest. And take a bath." She wrinkles her nose. Lizzie nods and wrinkles her nose, too.

There's a room off to the side of the hallway. It looks like an office, with bookshelves and a desk. Weirdly, there's a pool of water in the middle of the room. It rises a little bit out of the stone floor, and the water is right at the tippy edge, with a completely flat surface. It looks like glass.

"If you could put your finger in the middle of the pool?" the troll woman asks. "Just give the surface a little tap, enough to make some ripples."

I wipe my hand on my pants, making sure it doesn't have any crumbs on it; then I lean over as far as I can and boop the water. The surface ripples, and then the weirdest thing happens. I see Mom's face in the water. She's awake and sitting on the couch at home reading a book. Dad is next to her with his reading glasses at the tip of his nose, a newspaper spread out on the coffee table in front of them. Then I walk by and they both say something, but I can't hear what they say. The me in the pool says something to them and goes out the front door. A Lizzie chases after the me, and the door shuts behind them. The ripples stop and the images vanish.

"What," I say, "did I just see?"

"Our changelings," Lizzie says. "They're on their way back. And we're on our way home. Well, once Willy pulls the trigger."

"How did Mom and Dad not figure out those change-lings were fake?" I ask. "They were so weird!"

"When you encountered them, they were newly hatched," the troll woman says. "After becoming more familiar with your belongings and families, they would have been almost completely indistinguishable from the real you."

"Hatched?" I ask. "Like a little baby dinosaur Buck?"

The troll woman smiles. "They are actually trolls taking on human form. I can't have Topside getting all in a tizzy when I borrow their children. The trolls are only there for a short while. They take your place, and try to play as many violent video games and take as many martial arts classes as possible so they are somewhat trained for battle when they come back. The troll army is quite large. We've known this war is our destiny for quite some time."

They use video games to train?! What! That's the greatest thing I've ever heard!

"But what do the real kids do when they get here? That was the line of kids jumping into the Dumpster, right? They must have been totally flipping out."

"We keep them hypnotized," the troll woman says. "It's easier for everyone that way. They think they're going to the beach and we run a few quick tests to find our Halfling. Willy is the first to ever give us a positive."

Willy pumps her fist. "Yes!"

"Does Dad know he's a troll?" I ask. I can't believe that sentence just came out of my mouth.

Willy shrugs. "I guess you'll have to ask him when you get home."

"When *we* get home," I say. "*We* can ask him."

Everyone exchanges some uncomfortable looks, except for the Healer, who is spitting into his hands and rubbing them all over the scratches on my legs.

"Come here," Willy says, and she takes my hand. She leads me through a door behind the desk. Everyone else follows us. The door opens right onto a catwalk . . . a metal bridge spanning an enormous cavern. Below us are a zillion trolls. I can't tell exactly what they're doing, but they are definitely busy. It looks like they're making stacks of cannonballs on one end of the cavern. A bunch are on computers in another section. And in the middle there's something that looks a bit like a giant telescope. It's pointing up and out of a hole open above us. The night sky glitters through the hole.

"You see all those trolls?" Willy asks, leaning over the railing. I nod. "I'm their leader now," she says simply. "They've been waiting for me."

I give her the Lizzie Blinks. "But. What do you know about waging a war against gnomes? I mean, no offense, but you're still in elementary school. The Troll Queen is their leader."

"I am now the advisor to the leader," the troll woman says, and duh, Buck. Of course. This woman is the Troll Queen. Just because her crown isn't made of bones doesn't mean it means nothing.

"You're . . . ," I say, and my voice trails off. She nods and smiles.

"I have been the Troll Queen for a very long time," she says. "Since I was younger than Willy." Well, *that's* not in any of the books.

"B-but . . . ," I stammer. "I can't just leave you here, Willy. What would Mom say? What would Dad say?"

"Well, we could leave the changeling there," Willy says, looking at me intently. "What do you think?"

What do I think? I think this is all nuts! I thought this was MY adventure. I thought I was going to save the world. And now I'm being sent home while Willy becomes the hero? How can she wield the mace when I can't? We're both Halflings, aren't we? My bottom lip starts to quiver and I'm too tired to care. I look at Lizzie and I can't even find the words to say what I'm thinking because I'm not even sure what I'm thinking. Just that this doesn't seem very fair, and I've worked so hard, and almost been killed a million times, and Harold Macinaw, who I loved for so long, turned out to be a real jerk and then he was bleeding everywhere. . . . The crackers in my stomach start roiling.

"I need," I start, and then I ralph over the edge of the catwalk, splattering some poor trolls below.

"You need a bed," the Troll Queen says. "We'll finish this conversation later." She takes me by the arm and I basically fall asleep while I'm crying and walking and puking.

When I open my eyes I have no idea how many hours or days have passed. I have no idea what time it is. For a second I don't even remember where I am. There's a figure sitting at the end of the bed, and I think it might be Mom.

"Mom?" I say. My voice sounds like a frog.

"No, Marty McFly, it's me," Willy says.

I push myself up in bed and lean back on the pillows. My head is pounding and my mouth tastes like a Dumpster smells. I close my eyes and then open them. "You're really staying here?" I ask.

"Not forever," she says. "Just until the war is over."

"Wars last for years, Willy," I say. "You'd know this if

you were old enough to take world history in school."

"I have to stay until the prophecy is completely fulfilled, Buck."

"No you don't. You can come home with me."

"And leave the trolls to be enslaved by the gnomes? No one else can make the mace work, Buck. Only the Chosen One."

"That's the dumbest thing I've ever heard," I say, crossing my arms over my chest. "Also, how come *I'm* not the Chosen One? We both have the same parents. And *I* can talk to rocks. I'm a rockmouth, you know."

"I'm a rockmouth, too, Buck!" she says, clapping her hands. "Isn't it cool? How do you think I knew to come find you? The rocks were in my head, talking about someone shouting orders to them, and it wasn't me. I had to go check it out."

Whoa. Willy's a rockmouth, too? *Whoa.*

"I know it's weird about me being the only one to make the mace work, but really, it's no dumber than anything in Macinaw's books," Willy continues. "It's just . . . how it is."

I hold up my hand. "Don't say his name." I close my eyes. How can I go home without Willy? I came here to *get* her.

"What if I stay, too?" I ask. "I might not be the Chosen

One, but I'm still a Halfling. There has to be something helpful I can do. I don't think you understand the journey I've been on to find you, Willy. It was just like a book or a movie, except kind of worse in a lot of ways. I've been so scared and confused, and nothing turned out the way I thought it should. But it was still a mission, you know? This was my yellow brick road. I was out trying to find horcruxes. I did the Kessel Run in less than twelve parsecs— all to find you, Willy. I can't just go home now." I pull the crumpled book cover from my back pocket and hand it to her. "I found this. I thought it was a message from you to come save you."

Willy takes the cover and looks at it. She looks up at me and chews her bottom lip, finally looking like the Willy I know. "I did write this," she says. She takes the pencil out from behind her ear and fills in the smeared words.

Troll queen has us

were going up a mountain

Please send help

"I wrote it because I didn't know what was happening and I was so scared. I was able to resist the hypnotizing for little bits of time, and so I'd kind of wake up along the journey, and I'd be super-freaked out. I wrote this hoping that somehow you would find it and save me. Sorry it got all messed up." She hands it back and I put it in my pocket.

"It's not your fault it got all messed up," I say. "It was super-smart for you to leave it for me, even if you did ruin my book." I shove her shoulder playfully. She grins. Then her face gets really serious.

"I'm staying, Buck. I have to see this through. The trolls kept searching for the answer to the prophecy for some time, even after the gnomes stole the unicorn and tried to claim the prophecy as their own. I have to be the one to pull the trigger on that weapon out there. We're going to beat those mean gnomes, and the trolls are going to finally be free."

"But aren't you worried about getting hurt?" I say. "*I'm* worried you're going to get hurt."

"Oh, please," Willy says, rolling her eyes. "All I'm doing is pulling a trigger because some mystical thing says I have to. The trolls are doing all the hard work. They've been doing it for years. Believe me, they'd pull that trigger if they could. I don't know why a Halfling has to do it."

"Why can't I do it?" I ask.

"I didn't write the book, Buck. I don't know." She gives me a half smile.

"This isn't a book," I say, giving her a half smile back.

"Well then, there really aren't any rules, huh?" she says. "We just do what the fates tell us."

There's a knock on the door. Lizzie, Katya, and the Healer open it a crack and peek in. I motion for them to come in and they all sit on the bed.

"I'm sorry," I say.

"You do no things that are bad things," the Healer says, putting his claw on my hand. "But still I accept this sorry-ness."

"No," I say. "Lizzie. I'm sorry for being a jerk back there. I'm sorry for thinking you were weak or needed to be protected or whatever. It was dumb of me. How in the world did you and Katya and the Healer find this place?"

Lizzie grins. "We were walking through the forest and this huge dragon landed right in front of us. And Willy was on it! She said the rocks were all in a tizzy because a rock-mouth was in trouble and she was going to see if it was you. She called for another dragon and sent us here on the first one. So really, we didn't find her at all."

Katya nudges her with her shoulder. "You could have let him *think* we used our amazing tracking skills to find this place. Jeez." She rolls her eyes, but she's smiling.

"I found everyone!" Willy says, laughing. "I'm getting an A-plus at being the Chosen One!"

We all laugh, and it's so, so nice, having my sister and all my friends in one place, and in one piece. I think about

Smith and how he betrayed me. How he's probably in deep trouble right now, and how Macinaw is dead. I shiver. What a crazy adventure.

"So, what's next?" I ask. "If I stay? Can my changeling stay Topside with yours?" Willy is opening her mouth to say something when Lizzie interrupts.

"If you stay, I stay, Buck." She crosses her arms over her chest. "Someone has to make sure you don't go crazy and try to fight the whole war yourself."

I smile sheepishly. "But I thought you were ready to go home," I say. "I thought you were tired of this place; trying hard not to be tired of me." I look at my hands, not knowing what else to say.

Lizzie pulls me to her in a one-armed hug. "Turns out that once I got some food and rest I wasn't so worried about getting home right away. Well, that and knowing that Willy is in charge."

Willy grins. "And once you saw that your changeling was eating kelp and kale while you were eating cookies and peaberry jam . . ."

"What?! There are *cookies*?" I look up and pretend to be mad. Everyone snickers. "So we're staying, then?" I ask Lizzie. She nods. Willy nods. "And you?" I ask Katya.

"I must be a troll at heart, troll," Katya says, and punches me in the leg a little too hard. "We're a team, aren't we? We're all in this together, yeah?"

"Well, okay, then," I say, standing and rubbing my leg. My heart feels like it might burst from my chest—not in a scared way, but in an excited way. "What's first on the agenda?"

"I guess I have a war to start," Willy says with a rueful smile.

"I'll help," I say, "but can I take a shower first?" Everyone gives vehement nods and we all laugh again. "So you're really doing this?" I say to Willy. "For real?"

She nods. "Looks like gnome-a-geddon is only just beginning."

"Yeah," I say with a snort. "But will it be as good as the book?"

Acknowledgments

This book was almost not a book. It started out with a great bang and then . . . it faltered. It languished. It ended up in a drawer, cast away as an idea that was almost good, but just not good enough. Then, Ammi-Joan Paquette sent me an email. "How are the gnomes?" she asked. I wasn't sure what to say, so I didn't say anything. Then another email, and a few months later, another.

"How are the gnomes?"

"How are the gnomes?"

And finally, I opened the drawer. I spread out the pages. I reread what had been gathering cobwebs. How *were* the gnomes? It was time to find out.

My eternal thanks go to Joan for her quiet persistence over

the years. And a huge hurrah to Karen who saw a proposal about gnomes and trolls and said "Yes!" instead of "What?!" My thanks also go to everyone who read early chapters and early versions of this book. Joshua McCune, Bethany Hegedus, Sara Kocek, Vanessa Lee, E. Kristin Anderson, P. J. Hoover, Jodi Egerton, Anna Staniszewski, Timothy, Benjamin, Jack, Graciela, Julia, Daniel, and everyone else. Thank you!

I must of course thank my long-suffering children, Samuel, Georgia, and Isaac. I am always forcing them to make their own mac and cheese while I put on my headphones and writewritewrite. I am also always asking annoying questions like, "If I say 'poop smoothie,' is that too gross?" or "If I say 'elevenses,' do you know what I'm talking about?" Thanks, you guys, for always answering thoughtfully and for not burning down the house.

And last, but as far from least as possible, thank you to Shannon. Thank you for taking me to unimaginable worlds every day. I am fully, completely, unceasingly under your spell.